Gisèle Pineau was born in Paris in 1956, to
Guadeloupian parents. She has been living in the
West Indies (Martinique, Guadeloupe) since 1970.

Michael Dash is professor of French at the University
of the West Indies, Kingston, Jamaica.

the drifting of spirits
gisèle pineau

Translated by Michael Dash

Ǫ

First published in Great Britain by Quartet Books Limited in 1999
A member of the Namara Group
27 Goodge Street
London W1P 2LD

Originally published in France as *La Grande Drive des Esprits*

A catalogue record for this book is available from the
British Library

ISBN 0 7043 8101 X

Phototypeset by F.S.H. Ltd
Printed and bound in Great Britain by Cox & Wyman,
Reading, Berks

A Fernand

Contents

Time for Going Around

I

A Moment in Time

Léonce's life could have gone smoothly. In 1932, he was nearing twenty. He was a good-looking black brother with a muscular chest shaped from working in the fields. All the locals respected the way he embraced hard work and the good fortune that prevailed in his life. If women never flocked to him, it was because he dragged around a physical handicap from birth. A club-foot, if the truth be told, which gave him away from the furthest distance, in the darkness of day's end and in the wee hours of rainy mornings. He was renamed Kochi! No one really knows where this name came from. But everyone took to it with such ease that it stuck to Léonce, never to leave him again.

At that time, Myrtha was sixteen years old. Her face long and narrow, a soft coffee-colour. Her eyes flashed with the fire of suns. A slender body which displayed for all to see its hills and valleys, contours in a landscape never before seen under heaven. The arch of her back, her rounded hips, her bottom curved like a Spanish jar and her long tapering legs tugged at Léonce's heart. Then he would stare at his club-foot, the sole cause of his misery, a deep chasm of regret in which the anxieties of his heart and the bitter, mocking despair of his deformity tore at each other like dogs.

'Good God! I'm a man after all!' he said to himself.

'KOCHI! That's your name! Look at your foot, you upstart!' replied a wretched voice from deep within him.

Every day, Myrtha would pass his way bearing a bucket of water on her head. Her hips rose and fell, rolling under a band of red cloth. And Léonce, lying in a ditch, could do no more than admire this beauty, his nose in the grass, choking with passion.

'After all, I am a man!'

'A man!' croaked the wicked voice, crushing his

slightest longings. 'You are forgetting your foot! She will laugh in your face. Poor wretch, your tastes are unreasonable! You will only look bad beside her!'

It was grief from the beginning. Lying on her back, her legs spread wide, his mother, Ninette, agonised for one night and half a morning. Léonce emerged foot first, almost killing the poor woman. She screamed, struggling like a sow being slaughtered. So much so that in town many a person made the sign of the cross, commended her to the hands of the Lord and hastened to bury her six foot deep in their minds. But God is good and, that morning, death which was awaiting her left the darkness of her hut un-accompanied. The child was born with a caul and endowed with a club-foot. Papa Sosthène's face fell, troubled at the sight of both these peculiarities. To be born with a caul is to automatically possess super-natural powers. It is to open the gateway to the spirits who roam at the edge of the earth. It is to deal with the dead, to listen to words from the other world and to see beyond the visible. Urged on by her husband, Ninette applied a battery of fail-safe remedies whispered to her by a toothless old woman who had – it was said – protected many children born with a caul against the all-powerful drifting spirits. With great care and infinite patience, she put the caul out to dry on a bleached-out rock in the yard. When the sun had finished its job, she pounded the caul until it was reduced to a fine dust, which she fed to the child in small spoonfuls. Finally, she attached a pentacle of virgin parchment to his neck, said a series of novenas and dragged herself on her knees through countless churches in Guadeloupe. The caul eaten, the gift disappeared. Ninette did not suffer as much in giving birth to the younger children. Without the slightest wince, she brought forth in the following two years a son and a daughter whom she named Hector and Lucina. Afterwards, she lost a last child, in her sixth month. Then her body fell silent, no longer producing any kind of fruit. However, Sosthène was not lacking in desire. He had perfected a style of movement with his hips the like of which you could not imagine. Each and every night, a rich flood of semen coursed through Ninette's body, which docilely opened to his probings and never rejected his passion. Sosthène – God have mercy on him since he is no longer with us today – was a hard worker, a kind father, a good man at heart. But his head would turn so quickly each time the scent of woman reached his nostrils or a skirt wiggled before his eyes. His entire body would grow stiff. All thoughts of Ninette, his lawful wife, would fly zing! right out of his brain. And between his taut thighs the offending organ would rise, not hesitating to show him the direction he should take. Sosthène loved Ninette. Alas, his dreams of absolute fidelity could not withstand temptation. Of course, he pulled himself together after having fun, but too late, and his indiscretions drove him wild. No sooner had their bellies become swollen than the pregnant beauties would begin to make demands: a place to live, housekeeping money, education, shoes, school-books...Should Sosthène have to pay so dearly for one tiny moment of pleasure? Was he to blame because his seed would always fall on distressingly fertile fields? And what proof was there that these children who were put on his account were really of his making? Ninette curled her lip but did not make a scene when her husband's betrayals came screaming and cursing before her doorstep. All kinds of females were thoughtlessly laid by Sosthène because of his irresistible charm: tall chabines with mouths full of foul language, small black girls with bottoms round like calabashes, mulattas with soft flesh and ivory complexions. They all succumbed to temptation. They lay with him without question wherever he found them, lifting their skirts at the same time to receive the offering from the ill-fated male. The poor fellow could never understand his way with women. He did not force them, no way. So then, tell me, why this anger after the act, these unwarranted recriminations, since he promised nothing, neither paradise, nor marriage, nor allowance! As for Ninette, she would lock the house tight and then set out in vain to find some work to do, while Sosthène, hidden behind his Bible, asked the good Lord for forgiveness. He prayed with spectacular enthusiasm in order that the Devil incarnate should leave his yard as quickly as possible. But they were bitches, these women who were screaming outside. They had not come all this way to merely converse with the blackened boards of a locked-up house. They therefore got their revenge as best they could, flinging rocks at the zinc roof, defiling the garden, pulling up the stalks of chives, picking the fruits before they ripened and crushing the young plants underfoot. Once a capresse more bitter than a mad dog crushed pepper in the water jar. No, these women who came to harass Sosthène did not know when to stop. You would never have thought they were mothers of children. Mercifully, they were chased away by other, even more diabolical, creatures – succubi, she-devils with cloven feet, werewolves – and night did not find them in the yard. However, their screams returned with sleep, their curses arose in the twists and turns of dreams and their promises of doom gave rise to nightmares.

Léonce was seven when he set out for the first time for primary school. He went barefoot, proud of his starched shirt and his sharply pleated khaki shorts. His skull had been shaved with glass from a broken bottle. And deep in his pocket he held on to a piece of stale cassava that his mother had slipped him. In the past, the mouth was the domain of wit. No one cared whether you were touchy or thin-skinned. People loved to give nicknames and create new identities for others. So imagine this godsend of a foot, extraordinary enough to make she-devils shudder. This twisted foot, complete with its toes miserably clinging to the earth. This heel held taut by the stiff leg. This limping gait, funny enough to make your belly hurt. He learned to respond to the nickname he had been given and hid his sorrow behind a sweet disposition. And this is how, from the first time he encountered others, a bitter laugh took hold of his insides, ate away at his stomach, flattened his pride and made him look on the black girls, the little chabines and the little Indian girls from a great, great distance.

'Kochi! That is your name!' whispered the bitter voice. 'Deal with that curse! Look if you dare!'

At twelve, the boy abandoned the quest for education and followed Papa Sosthène to the vegetable garden. With each season, he tensed his muscles and everyone noticed that Ninette's oldest was from a strong breed. In truth, it was to shed his disability that he wielded the hoe, the machete and the shovel with so much determination. He knocked off more work than those who were unimpaired. The latter stood with their mouths agape, watching this challenge defiantly thrown each day in the face of destiny. Wiping their brows, they would say: 'Kochi, you are really and truly strong! Damn, you make the earth cry out for mercy! Your yams are more beautiful than young black virgins!'

At sixteen, after the hurricane of 1928, he went off all alone to sell his produce at the big vegetable market in Pointe-à-Pitre. He left early morning by boat and returned in the evening with a pile of coins in a huge handkerchief deep in his pocket. He really had a feel for it and made use of a clever technique. He would simply place his body in the middle of the tubers of yam and, his club-foot displayed like the prize jewel of his crop, he would attract religious types brimming with compassion, kind souls eager to do a good turn and also nosy characters with fat purses. At eighteen, by dint of patience and thrift, he bought a hillside from an old mulatto in dire straits who was being pursued by bailiffs all over Guadeloupe.

11
The Face of Love

'Look at your foot, Kochi!' said the voice from the shadows.

You have land and good fortune, thought Léonce, but you still need the crowning glory. A loving woman with a brand-new belly waiting to be filled with kids. A wife coming and going in a home echoing with the noises of a family.

'Get off it, Kochi! Be happy with selling your yams and forget skirt tails! You will never find a woman to feel your prick!...'

Ninette's first-born was her pride and joy as well as a source of sorrow. Her pride and joy because he worked like a dog to turn the land he had bought to account. He did not drink rum, roll dice, play cards or any other foolishness invented by men to drain pockets and squander the few pennies from their produce. And he had, if you please, the graciousness of a senator even if the school had no memory of his setting foot in it. Nevertheless, Ninette was grief-stricken. Léonce hid himself from the sight of women while desire tingled deep within him like ticks travelling along the back of a grazing bull.

A bucket of water on her head, her backside swinging from side to side with her swaying gait, Myrtha went about her business, not giving a thought to a certain Léonce, who began, because of her, to drift precariously close to the edge of lustful folly. He undressed her in his dreams. He saw droplets of water splash from the bucket and roll down her luminously satin skin, like pearls of rainwater. He sprawled out on the grass, like a dog which had fallen in the midst of a lair of mad ants. He knew by heart the curvaceous shape of his idol. His hand wildly traced its beloved curves. He felt his way like a blind man using his fingers to see, groping, hesitating, weighing, and he would take her full in his mouth like a fruit without seeds. He took her off to his hillside, to this land all paid for in cash which would say each day: 'The promise of a good harvest, that is my name!' He ended up laying her in the grass and bestowed on her that burning sap that was eating him up inside.

'You worthless fellow! Take a look at your foot! She will spit you out!...Do you really believe that this black beauty already beyond the reach of fellows with no defect whatsoever, this black woman whose body is a virgin landscape where hollows, mounds and flat clearings rise and fall, will want a hastily put together male? Do you believe that a cripple like you, whom everyone calls Kochi, can one day scale these heights and tread on this unexplored continent? An exercise in futility! Around her, a million and one roosters flap their wings, prance and preen, lying in wait for her virginity. Take care of your yams, Kochi, and dismiss from your mind thoughts of this land which will never harbour you!'

By then love had sown its seeds in Léonce's heart. He no longer ate, no longer slept, no longer knew the way to his garden. And his yams, from neglect, rotted in the earth. He no longer took the early boat to convert the fruits of his labour into cash. His space remained empty in the big market of La Pointe. People inquired after him, but no one could offer any sort of explanation. He tried to turn his back on this great sorrow which tore away at his soul. But Myrtha, in her nakedness, turned and twisted in his brain. He hoped once more to take charge of his daily existence with hope and patience. Alas, the beauty's comings and goings consumed his every waking moment.

Ma Ninette was on the alert, knowing full well that a club-foot did not completely cancel out the power of a man and especially of a true son of Sosthène. After a sleepless night, when the boy's tears made her heart sizzle in her chest more sharply than meat browned in an old stew-pot, she decided to deal once and for all with this persistent wound that ordinary care could not heal. Passion became too excruciating for his body. Léonce shrivelled to skin and bone like a Good Friday, became more bitter than a green cerasee and his heart broke like the ground in dry season, cracking and moaning under the sun's lashes. Ninette raised the matter with Sosthène. He did not listen to her; he was chewing the remains of a prayer while shutting the door in the face of the shrieks of a former partner who was demanding, again and again, some money for her bastard son, who had gone off to become a soldier in France. So Ninette, like a faithful dog, began to spy on her Léonce, following him everywhere. Courage and love gave his bones strength even if his body was worn out with fatigue. The boy no longer ate or slept, no longer knew who he was. He knew only one thing: the time Myrtha walked past. The angle of the sun in the sky never deceived him. No sooner had he thrown his wretched body into the ditch than his beloved would appear. Ninette had seen many beauties come and go... So what! She saw in her nothing more than just another of the ordinary black girls that were a dime a dozen in the Guadeloupean countryside. She shook her head angrily when she found her Léonce dumbfounded, refusing to look away from the path abandoned by his queen. You could say that Myrtha never really left this spot. It was as though her spirit haunted this path. The trees seemed to acknowledge her presence, the birds to sing her praises and the rocks to soften their sharp edges.

Ninette first of all had to get her facts straight. You never know! Sosthène had fathered so many kids throughout the countryside... Mercifully, Myrtha was born on the other side of Grande-Terre. It was only a couple of years since her parents had settled with their dreams at the edge of the town. They lived in an antiquated cabin perched lopsidedly on four river stones. The boards were worn out by sun and rain, the zinc roof eaten away by rust and the bottoms of doors greedily gnawed at by the jaws of time. Ninette almost turned back. Was she not forcing the hand of destiny? Good Lord! Should she facilitate this union?

Ma Boniface, Myrtha's mother, was a big red woman, heavy in the hip. Myrtha represented the beginning and the end of her progeny. That is to tell you how passionately she fussed over her only daughter! Most certainly, she would not have given her to just any fellow without possessions or a proper education. Pa Mérinés, with whom she lived, claimed to be the descendant of a true-blooded Congo who had arrived long after slavery. He despised the local blacks, boasting of his own African ancestors, who had known neither chains nor beatings nor punishment at the stake. He proclaimed himself free despite his poverty and his not so heavy meals... More free than those who had kept their fetters, chains which they continued to feel just as you forever sense a limb that was gangrenous, amputated and buried. He was a man of ebony skin, dry, with thick corded veins snaking across his huge hands. His teeth glistened, firmly fixed in purple gums which he displayed occasionally, when he burst into laughter, exerted force with his hoe or bit into squares of breadfruit. Ninette found them both in their yard as if they were expecting her visit. She swallowed hard and waded in:

'A good evening to you, ladies and gentlemen! This is why I have come: my eldest is dying of love for your dear child. He is wasting away. He has never said two words to her but, night and day, day and night, for years now, he is beside himself because of this passion, which is too demanding for his constitution. My Léonce is a hard worker who is not in the habit of chasing skirts, gambling, drinking rum with friends. Since he turned eighteen, he has been the owner of land acquired by his labour. He is one of that breed of black men which you no longer find anywhere.'

Boniface's heart recoiled at Ninette's flattering approach. She was faced with the one and only prize of her loins being stolen from her and handed over in matrimony to some fellow whom she had not chosen. She did not even glance at the female petitioner and continued mechanically shelling her pigeon peas, her mind afflicted by much agitation. As for Mérinés, he seemed more deaf than someone a hundred years old. Listlessly filing the blade of his machete, he spat on the ground. Then, he cast an empty look at the woman who was relentlessly listing the outstanding virtues of her son. Ninette got it off her chest, fell silent and waited. In the yard, you could hear only the dull sound of pigeon peas cascading down into the cracked calabash. The countryside seemed to stretch out around them.

'And what fault could he have, this perfect man who hides from the gaze of honest folk?' the father let fly behind a gob of green spittle.

The go-between mother, though she was expecting this response, was seized with trembling. For a moment only silence greeted Mérinés' question. Then the hint of a smile from Boniface, who coughed, chuckled and nodded to her partner to thank him for his insight. So, without beating around the bush, Ninette confessed to the deformity. But, before this piece of news could sink in, presto, she had donned her lawyer's robes, pleading the case for her eldest son; in his defence he owned a profitable and beautiful piece of land, a whole hillside as an offering to Myrtha...almost a white Creole's property! In truth, you could find dozens of females who had set their sights on this promising future. Alas, Léonce had eyes only for this one. Ninette had not finished speaking when Myrtha appeared. Immediately, a hearty laugh burst from deep within Boniface's troubled soul and shattered the tension that had charged the country air.

'Ah ha! Who said you were ready to get married! And with a club-foot to boot! You're not going to be the girl walking arm in arm with a cripple, even if he owns the so-called property of a white Creole...But what does he believe, this creature! That my flesh and blood has come all this way to beckon to grief!...Oh no, you're not going to tie up your future and get married just for a piece of land! No one told them you were for sale...' Ma Boniface laughed loudly, like someone playing dice who has just lost his last penny in an unlucky move.

Myrtha placed her bucket of water on the beaten ground, adjusted the cloth around her hips, looked without laughing at Ma Ninette, who was sizing her up, and asked:

'Does this man already have a cabin to put a wife in?'

From that day, Boniface locked away her Myrtha deep in her cabin and went herself to fetch water from the fountain. Two-three days went by. A week seemed like ten centuries. And Léonce, poor fellow, agonising in the ditch of despair, lay in wait each morning, desperately hoping his beloved would pass by. Three-four weeks slipped by. And Léonce was definitely heading for his last breath. Not a day went by without Ninette dragging herself over to him and repeating the girl's words.

'"Does this fellow already have a cabin to put a wife in?" That's what she said to me, Léonce. Come on, get a hold of yourself! Grab your saw and your machete! Put aside zinc, planks and posts! Three weeks from now, with a helping hand, this cabin that she is asking for will be up!'

Finally, one fine morning, no one knows what wind blew, his mother's coaxing found its way into his head. Léonce jumped out of the ditch. He once more tasted food and little by little life found its way back to him along the path of hope that Ninette had traced.

III
A Slap of Humility

Without further ado Léonce left the world of spirits which had had a tight hold on him for some time. Myrtha no longer took the rocky path to fetch water. But hope nonetheless gave the fellow a sense of direction, pushed him forward and urged him to get a grip on life. He was to construct without delay the one condition demanded by his beloved. Contrary to the beliefs of his mother, Ninette, it was not his intention to build, hurry-hurry, some ordinary cabin in his spare time, with picked-up boards and 'That's fine! That can pass! That should do it! That should hold up!' A wretched cabin studded with bent nails, its rafters all wrong, decked out with only God knows what kind of roof tree and its framework at the mercy of hurricanes, dolled up with doors and windows without frames, and with an uneven floor. He wanted a superior kind of cabin, like those that the less fortunate see from afar, behind the foliage of ginger lilies, fire gingers and yellow or red helconia, across stretches of forbidden lawns. A cabin that you could not find any- and everywhere. A cabin worthy of Myrtha's bearing, with frills and fretwork prominently displayed. A master carpenter from Grande-Terre was recommended, a gentleman of solid reputation. The boy counted up the little money from his yams and decided, eventually, to undertake the journey.

And so it was that one fine morning, he pulled on his heavy white suit over his starched shirt, tied his black silk bow-tie and then put on the pair of boots made for him by Asson, a shoemaker madly in love with architecture. With great care, he had measured the length, width and height of the foot, and sweated for days on end in order to finish this masterpiece that would testify to his great talent. The special boot was equipped with a fifteen-centimetre heel crafted from a soft wood. On the front a double row of eyelets ran

vertically and across them snaked a tight lace. Léonce
still limped, but the leather was soft, well polished and,
dressed up like this, his deformity looked far more
presentable. A smell of perfume marked his passage,
spreading along the path: mille-fleurs, ilang-ilang,
lavender and patchouli. He no longer had anything in
common with the shadowy creature raving in the
ditch of unrequited love. That day when he presented
his perfumed self in the boat, the usual passengers
gazed at him with some respect, then began to
whisper among themselves, their hands over their
mouths, just as you might do in the presence of a
priest. Léonce made no effort to chat with anyone. He
preferred to look at the sky over which large masses of
torn clouds stretched, the sea which steered his fate
and Grande-Terre, where could be found La Pointe,
Sainte-Anne and the renowned master-builder who
would build the structure to house his future. He
walked the roads of the town and reached La Darse,
where he got into a vehicle half filled with passengers.
After going every which way up and down hillsides,
he got off at Grands-Fonds. A fellow passing by
pointed out to him the workshop of the famous
carpenter.

Master Paulius, an affable man with the gift of the
gab, let himself be called by neighbours, relatives and
friends: Ti Bouboule. He had a reputation which
stretched over his native Grande-Terre, made its way
through all of Basse-Terre, swelled in Saint Lucia and
eventually got lost in continents never crossed by

people from around here. There was not a single soul who did not appreciate – at least through hearsay – the massive dwellings he had put up with skill and know-how for a few families. All about, workmen copied his designs and his fancy fretwork, but, if the truth be told, without any success. He alone had the know-how. The wood bore his signature. And you could always identify the original from among the multitude of copies. He had his own way of fashioning the beams, of fixing the pegs and of wielding the mallet. He gauged his angles with the naked eye, marked out the frame freehand and sculpted, in his workshop, brackets which were the envy of the entire colony.

When Léonce found himself facing Paulius, his lips froze and the words stuck in his throat. This living monument to carpentry took a good look at the special boot, the white drill suit, the shirt, the bow-tie and Léonce's tormented face. Exasperated, he began to tap the palm of his hand with a grooving-plane. He was used to seeing a stream of hopeless young fellows who were after a position as apprentice, in the undisclosed hope of stealing the gift that guaranteed his success. Until that morning, none had turned up dressed like this. When Léonce began to divulge his ambitions, Ti Bouboule's pockmarked face crinkled and a big laugh swelled within him. 'A two-room cabin! Ah! Ah! Ah! And in what country will you be erecting this absurdity?' The master's face swelled with laughter. His wide-open mouth produced an un-sympathetic guffaw that succeeded in deflating

Léonce completely. The carpenter immediately summoned his folks. Time for a good laugh! Everyone just had to hear these absurd instructions. A two-room cabin! Which he would have the privilege of erecting… He! A masterbuilder with his solid reputation. A two-room house… Hold on! With all the trimmings: the unusual fretwork, the Venetian ornamentation, the sculptured columns, the frills and this and that. A two-room house, you hear!, to be set down on some wretched hillside, on the other side of salt river, behind God's back, in a country ill-suited to vehicles. A two-room house, just that! Forming a circle around a Léonce cringing within his jacket, the Creole gathering, which loved to laugh and gesticulate, bent double, as if they had an attack of colic, arms and legs flying to and fro, and laughed so loudly that bits of food mingled in a stream of chewed tobacco and overproof rum. No, my friends, as far as the people of Grands-Fonds could remember, never had anyone insulted Ti Bouboule like this. 'A two-room cabin! Do you see that written on my face? Get away, you rascal! Leave my sight! Go back to your neck of the woods and find a skilled carpenter who, if he so desires, will copy my style and will perhaps satisfy your fancy tastes!'

This is how Léonce felt a stinging slap of humility and went off to secure the services of Sipolin Bravard, who erected on the hillside the only house in Haute-Terre which faces the sea and, sometimes, pierces two-three clouds.

IV
With Hand on Heart

Myrtha would leave home only when escorted by her mother, the unbending Ma Boniface. Already standing on the hillside, upright like a first communion table, the cabin awaited her arrival. Ah! Sipolin Bravard had, you could say, outdone Master Paulius. From every nook and cranny of Haute-Terre, they came to see the masterpiece, to marvel and to congratulate Kochi, who, with hope in his heart, spent his days cleaning around the house, planting shrubs and lots of flowers. Encouraging words flew from one mouth to another:

'You don't need to wear yourself out like that, Kochi! She will most certainly come...Any woman would die for that kind of house...'

'Who could stand in the way of your pulling off this miracle?'

'The Lord moves in mysterious ways, son!'

Words of advice too came tumbling forth:

'Put the lilies over here, the heliconias over there!'

'Plant this coconut tree right here! This guava tree lower down!'

'She will love you, Kochi! Your heart really deserves that! Pay no attention to your old club-foot, forget it!'

'Move this orange tree a little more to the right! It is too close to the house!'

'No lie, my friend, you could say you planted the garden of Eden here...'

Léonce would smile, sometimes.

And then, one heaven-blessed day, Myrtha made her own way up the hill. Ma Boniface was drained of her strength because of an illness which had suddenly taken hold of her bones. So her daughter escaped. As fate would have it, no one saw. On that day some folks were taken up with some task or other, others were relaxing during their siesta or, tired of waiting for their much desired damsel, spent their time in idle chatter, close by the shops.

Our friend had acquired an ox. Partly to fill the emptiness in his life, partly to invest his money. Whatever the reason, he pampered the animal as if he were dealing with a thoroughbred from America. He would talk to it better than he would to a friend, and would stroke it for hours, because his loneliness weighed so terribly on him, in spite of the many gossips who, their arms folded, sniggered behind his back. He sat up for nights on end watching, from his hilltop, the comings and goings of people and the dim lights trembling in the darkness of the town. Alas, what else could he do other than hang on for dear life to this branch of hope that his mother had created for him to survive, and dream of this excessive love which tortured him mercilessly, leaving him alone in the dark, hollow-eyed, his body on edge. Never!, he had sworn to himself, would he even go near to Myrtha's cabin. You understand, if he had decided to go there and his beloved had wickedly made fun of him ... What was left for him to cling to, if a burst of laughter were to deflate his ambitious plans?

When the sound of Myrtha's crystal voice was heard behind the love-stricken fellow, a mighty shudder overwhelmed him. Then, a whirling wind gushing from the bowels of the earth blew across his club-foot, made its way up his leg, shook his prick, spread into his chest, froze his arms and mashed up his brain. He fell, bap! out cold, senseless amidst a bundle of yams he had just dug up. The ox, who knew about the whole affair because of his master's repeated confidences, did not budge. Let the breed of creatures who stand upright sort out their business by themselves! he thought. And, oblivious like eternity, the animal continued quietly chewing his cud, while his tail flicked across his haunches, which were being attacked by a swarm of blue flies searching for food. Kochi lay on the ground. He seemed to be suffering from sunstroke, but his mind was alert. His head was teeming with insults:

'Big fool! You really deserve your name! She comes up the hill. She stands before you and you bite the dust! Get up, for Christ's sake, she is standing there! Up! like the man you claim to be! What kind of monkey business is this! At least acknowledge her! Present her with your greetings! Bid her welcome!'

But the little voice inside, wicked and evil, sapped his will:

'You're not a man, my friend! Look at your foot! Who would want you? This beauty beyond compare! What do you believe, wretch? That your future hangs on a throw of dice!'

That's why, his body in a complete mess, Léonce no longer moved, barely breathed, and did not open his eyes.

'What's the matter with you? I was told you were dying of love, it's true! You're dead!' she said, blowing on his unresponsive face.

He heard each word, but did not move the tiniest hair. Admit it, it is pleasant to lie, eyes closed, body still, enjoying the warmth of a soft breeze which makes the skin tingle and tickles your nostrils as well as your eyelashes. The sun blazed down, hard. His face glistening with sweat, Léonce felt once more the caressing breath and the soothing balm of his beloved's voice:

'My God, he is dead!' A cool hand touched the fellow's lips. Then another, soaked in water from the bucket, mopped his brow. Then he opened his eyes. And he immediately closed them, blinded by that divine face so close to his. Myrtha laughed before scolding him:

'What kind of man are you?' She saw the evidence of the shrubs and also the don't-give-a-damn ox, the piles of yams and the flowers which stretched out their cone-like corollas to catch the gardener's every word. 'So this is how you greet visitors. Well, I am going...' She pretended to get up. Léonce took a tight hold of her hand. The girl burst out laughing. The ox winked and snorted. Then, his eyelids still lowered, Léonce summoned up his courage and asked, in a low voice filled with both hope and fear:

'Did you climb the hill to give me your reply? Will you accept my mother's proposal? If the answer is no, free yourself and leave without looking back! If it is yes, place your other hand on my heart...It belongs to you for ever.'

When she heard these beautiful words, Myrtha's nipples hardened under her blouse. Ladies and gentlemen, at that very moment, our beauty realised that the man involved was a poet for goodness' sake, the sentimental type, from that group of fellows who know how to turn a phrase and use the French language with know-how. She had come out of curiosity to look on this cabin about which the whole of Haute-Terre was talking. In truth and in fact, our beauty had always dreamed of being a married woman in a brand-new house. To tell you what was really in her mind, love had not left the slightest mark on her heart. That very morning she did not give a damn about the fellow who was said to be consumed with passion. She did not attempt to free herself. But neither did she put her hand on the heart which was beating so hard in the poor fellow's insides. Her life was in the balance between her two hands; leave or remain until the end of her days. Go off and conquer the world or stop here, once and for all, on this quiet hillside. Await another man, another love, or adjust to this one. He did not dare lift up his eyes to her, he was swollen with passion and would drag, throughout his entire life – unless the Virgin Mary herself appeared – this club-foot to the accompaniment of sniggers and pity. She had another look at him. He was blessed with a handsome, a kind face, this Léonce. A decidedly nice fellow. A hard worker, that was obvious. The soul of a poet... She looked closely at the cabin with all its doors wide open, like so many inviting and expectant arms. She took in the road below the hill, the town and its string of wretched cabins with zinc roofs speckled with rust, and far off on the sea, the canoes of fishermen rowing off to La Pointe with its halo of grey, artificial clouds. Only then did she place her hand on Léonce's heart.

Climbing the hill a little earlier, the girl thought of her mother, who was dying. She was racked with doubt. Had the obstacles created by Ma Boniface to prevent the hypothetical union unleashed the forces of the supernatural? On this day with no one as witness, had some spirit led her there, so that a prophecy could be fulfilled? Since Boniface fell ill, Pa Mérinés was resentful of Myrtha, saying that she was the cause of this mysterious illness for which there was no cure. He spent from morning to evening at the dying woman's bedside, slumped over, eyes half-closed, hands tirelessly consoling the now wasted body of his spouse, who was sucking away at the final moments of her life.

Love had not yet clamped its jaws shut on Myrtha. But, as we all know, the heart is not reason's twin brother. They did not come out of the same woman's womb. As children, they did not have fun together playing hopscotch. The heart is a snake which tastes all the fruit of the earth and gobbles up the tender flesh of a naseberry just as greedily as the poisonous berry of the manchineel tree. Reason is more tasteless than a dish of christophines, paler than a chabine nun cloistered in her Saint-Joseph-de-Cluny convent...

Myrtha's childhood was not fun and games. A sneaking memory made her understand that two identical women took care of her as a baby. She also remembered a merciless hurricane from the other side of the island that blew the first house of her step-father Mérinés right into the air, like a woman's skirts

31

lifted for all to see. When she was eight or nine years an old stingy mulatto woman took her in. For a daily dish of breadfruit, the cruel foster mother worked her to the bone while depriving her of primary schooling. Sometimes, Myrtha thought of those evenings of hunger and weeping when she begged the Lord to send her back her mother. Just before she turned ten, Boniface finally turned up, with the same Mérinés blessed with poverty and a filthy cabin. On some nights, it rained through the gaping roof on to the smelly bed. 'The heavens must be more merciful elsewhere!' Ma Boniface would swear as they made their way, the cabin behind them, pulled along on a cart whose every joint creaked. One day Haute-Terre appeared at a bend in the road. Mérinés and Boni found the spot to their liking and the planter easy to deal with. It was the middle of the cane harvest. The factory rumbled and smoked. Myrtha turned fourteen. All day long she remained by herself in the old cabin that she detested more than anything else, busying herself with housekeeping, cooking and going to fetch water morning after morning from the standpipe in the town. One Sunday, in church, she swore she would live in a new house. Before the Lord God, Jesus Christ and the Virgin Mary, she made the vow she would marry the first man to make this dream come true. She would keep his house clean, fill it with flowers, dress it up with curtains, pack it with the required, fancy, well-polished furniture. She would do everything to deserve it! This is why, on that already long-gone day when Ninette revealed the virtues and the single imperfection of her son, Myrtha could not resist temptation. That very moment, come what may, she committed herself to the new house. She mounted that horse called destiny even before knowing her companion on the journey, how long it would last and where it would all end. It could well be that the needle of hope that now stitched together Léonce and herself held the promise of a fine piece of work...

Léonce felt the heat from Myrtha's hand. He opened his eyes and his gaping mouth displayed a perfect set of teeth. As he gradually realised that his dream had taken on the shape of reality, the fellow beamed. In response, Myrtha lowered her eyes. Léonce took delight in looking at her, his gaze caressing the contours and planes of this beloved face. Deep inside his brain, the small voice choked with rage, while the young girl's heart suddenly took flight. A wordless moment went by. And then the sky suddenly broke, like a dry calabash dashed against a rock. Rolling black clouds broke free from the horizon and darkened the broad daylight. The first drops of rain spattered the young people and then lashed them. They ran to the cabin, Myrtha's hand in Léonce's. The sudden anger of the heavens, which endured for some time as the favourite story of a few old folk from Haute-Terre, caused three canoes from Les Saintes to capsize. In the town's centre, eyes seeking answers from the good Lord, the ordinary people eager for some supernatural explanation already knew that in time to come there would be some reason for this wicked dry-season rain. They were not wrong. Later they were to discover that at the very instant when the sky drew dark, opened and broke its waters on to the earth, Boniface was uttering her last Christian sigh while Mérinés was hurriedly binding her hands with a rosary... But, in all honesty, was Boniface really a Christian? Do good people pass away in this kind of pain? Would they not find, under her bed, an enamel basin filled with rancid communion wafers and leaves for casting spells?

Despite the multitude of unnecessary words, the mouths that shut bap! when she went by, like jalousies caught red-handed in the act of snooping, and the love that swelled her heart, Myrtha wore mourning for her mother with great dignity. Mérinés had thrown her out of the house, accusing her of killing Boni by accepting the propositions of a cripple. So, quite naturally, Ma Ninette welcomed her under her roof. There was nothing wrong in it since Léonce was going to marry the orphaned girl. And, with great patience, the town hall and the church waited for the end of the customary period of grief in order to inscribe on the public register the conjoined names of Léonce and Myrtha. And on the hill, with its fancy frills and latticework, the new cabin also waited, counting the days that remained.

V
Love's Torment

1960. I was a young girl of seventeen at that time. The stamp of my newly acquired graduation diploma all over my face. My whole body racked with un-certainty, depending on the moment, as to the direction my future should take: classical literature, ethnology, political science...It was the long vacation.

I wandered aimlessly all over Guadeloupe, a Rolex camera slung over my shoulder − reward for my success − and, deep in my heart, the major project of an original picture-book of Creole houses. I scoured town and country. I went on foot, by cart, on bicycle. Snap! Snap! For posterity, I captured on film a number of cabins, the beautiful and the ugly, the young and the old, the gutted, the roofless, those painted the colours of the rainbow or scraped clean and grey, the abandoned ones.

One morning, I decided to go even deeper into the countryside. There I discovered − pure heaven for a budding photographer! − a cabin more than a hundred years old clinging like a maddened bat to the side of a green hill. Superb contrast! Powerful symbolism! Life and death united in a struggle to the death. I adjusted my Rolex, set the shutter. Snap! Snap! I made this uplifting yet depressing vision my own. At that very moment, behind me, an angry voice suddenly arose.

'Who are you? Whose permission did you ask for, eh? You've got it into your head to imitate the whites who come around to photograph the falls up there! You have no family! Where are you from? Who is your mama?'

Startled, almost tripping, I immediately turned around. It was an old red woman with wide hips. Her gums were studded with black stumps. On her head, which had never seen a comb, two old-fashioned twists bristled with sword-like pins. She sported a dirty dress, all torn and stained with banana sap. She was holding a small machete and her eyes chopped me into tiny pieces. Suddenly, for no apparent reason, her anger disappeared. Her hand relaxed. The machete landed at her mud-spattered feet. And serenity washed over her face glistening with sweat.

I imagined immediately that I had come upon a pristine, unadulterated kind of lunacy, that my feet had led me right before one of those creatures with neither head nor tail which went through life in the manner of mad ants. I felt like a maroon on the run just ahead of the pack. Glancing at my bicycle with one eye and at the so distant road with the other, I counted my steps, calculated how long it would take to cover the distance and tried a sidestep to the left. The old woman stopped me with a wave of her hand, which was neither a threat nor an entreaty. I stopped in mid-flight. Then, she began to speak. I listened to her, my heart swept away in a wild swirl. She raised her eyebrows and it was as if she was lifting the curtain behind which, trembling from having been caught, lay those three accomplices: the past, oblivion and memory. She drew a hand more shrivelled than an old passion fruit across her brow, criss-crossed with wrinkles. Forty years of suffering and regret settled in the hollow of her damp palm. She shook her head, laughed and pulled from her clothing a chewed-up cigarette stub which she stuck in the hollow of a tooth. Then she related, spread out, right there, her entire life. As for me, my eyes were bound by curiosity and my lips skewered by all the emotion that a young virgin with a diploma is capable of feeling.

... Her name was Barnabé. She had a man's Christian name just like her twin, Boniface. At the time, fathers liked to lighten the burden of their disappointment by bestowing on their girl children such titles. There was one, a certain Archibald, who became bitter as soon as his eyes fell on those two noisy bundles of flesh which were already a sign of: bubbies galore, periods and everlasting worries. Boniface and Barnabé were born at the time when families were huge. They had twelve blood brothers and five half-brothers, bitter fruit from Papa's wanderings. Their early childhood was spent clinging to Mama Lucie's breasts. They then became familiar with the girls' school in order to pick up some intellectual baggage, decipher the hieroglyphs of the sacred French language and receive blows from teacher's stick, doled out painfully on their out-stretched fingers. On Thursdays, they sat side by side on the benches of the presbytery for Catechism lessons. During vacation, they ran wild with their brothers over hills and flatlands, plunged into rivers and got lost in the everlasting sugar-cane fields. But one day, as fate would have it, their chests developed nipples that grew and grew and produced big bubbies, as awkward for them as they were attractive to the young boys who saw the prospect of other kinds of play. Father Archibald's face darkened. Oh, horrors! Suddenly, after a belly ache, they began to piss blood. Ma Lucie then told them the story of the curse put on women ever since the apple and the serpent. They learned to scrub their period cloths, which were soaking behind the house, under the almond tree, in basins of soapy water. That is how two women finally stood up straight in their father's house. Age seventeen, twenty, twenty-four... All the forbidden parties and the young bucks chased away one after the other like dogs without a home. However, the twins' bodies were already favoured by the caress of time, understood the wordless looks of the junior as well as the senior males. Their ears hungrily longed for those sweet-as-honey words that make you believe in heaven and make your skin tingle. Their mouths wilted because of the absence of love's torment, which steered clear of their eager appetites. But Archibald did not give a damn. The scoundrel swore by all the alabaster saints lined up in the church of our Lord that none of his virgins would invite brother dishonour in through the door. He made quite a fuss over this business, which had the tongues in the neighbourhood wagging. He stood watch and verified each month, with his own two eyes, the colour of the period cloths. Suitors continued to hover.

Go on, go on! Find a solution! What course is left open when that evil stepmother ill-luck puts down her load?

— Swallow, without blinking, like some blessed sacrament, life's reversals. Accept this terrible fate of perpetual virginity. And grow old before your time like French apples.

— Gaze, with jealousy secreted in your eye corner,

at the giddy females parading, after evensong, on the arms of the dashing young men. And drool with envy.

– And finger each evening the little bump of useless flesh, all the while thinking of their Jehovah's Witness neighbours, who would pass by each Sunday, repeating that decidedly the wages of sin are death.

The twin girls kept going round in circles in the cabin up to the day when…Miracle of miracles! Prayers were answered! Archibald was visited by a messenger. He was to leave without delay. Of course, he advised, warned, threatened. 'The boys will take over and stand guard over the women!' he said before setting out, a knapsack of rags over his shoulder. He turned around one last time and raised his hand. A wave of goodbye or a final warning? The mother wept. The twin girls poured out buckets of tears to fool the onlookers. But, on the inside, they were laughing like two she-devils that some unfortunate soul has just picked up in his carriage. The brothers came and went, turned and twisted, their eyes too distant from their sisters. They were overburdened by work in the fields, hunting, fishing and taking care of the domestic animals. That is when the fellows in the neighbourhood, greedy like a pack of rats before a fowl coop, found themselves facing a windfall. The mighty virgins first tasted the first course of compliments. And then, teeth bared, dazzled by the looking-glass that love is, flung themselves into illusion's nets. The orchids jealously locked away by Archibald were savagely plucked by mangoose gardeners. From pain was born the pleasure of mingled flesh. Night found the flushed girls leaving their soft beds to roll in a bed of grass with some chap whose looks really did not matter. Wash days found them at the river being worked over by overly fertile males. The mother saw nothing. The brothers came and went, paying no attention to the girls' behaviour. When the father returned, the mad cavorting stopped, just like that. Life took on once more its mournful pace. But the times of wrong-doing had sapped life's flow. The doomed sisters cast at each other looks of cattle on reprieve, waiting patiently in front of the doorway of the slaughterhouse. The mother realised but too late. She prepared for them with trembling hand a tea reputed to make women's eggs come down. All three began to hope for the return of the menstrual fluid which would wash away their sins. They prayed to the Virgin Mary, but did not dare to repeat to her the words that hummed in their bewildered minds. Alas, the eggs did not come down. To undo suspicion and fool their father, who was beginning to smell the breath of conspiracy encircling him, they poured chicken blood into the basins of soapy water where immaculate period cloths lay soaking. He opened his eyes, cocked his ear for the slightest sound and poked his nose in every corner. But everyone under his roof pretended to go about normally, kept their mouths shut and chewed on the thoughts of ill-luck and doom. Their brows were smooth and their bellies flat, so tight were they strapped down. Time went by, pursued by the weight of bad luck whose burden grew more heavy with each day.

So what were they to do? Take off! Exile themselves far from a future filled with scorn, hatred and dishonour!

Run away before being chased away by their outraged father!... That may well have been the only course. They therefore left the district where they were born without taking the smallest bundle of clothes, in order not to arouse the suspicions of the neighbours. They covered all of Grande-Terre, bellies banded down in the frocks of fake virgins. They walked for kilometres without exchanging a single word, without the slightest complaint, tear, squeak. To what end! Thoughts swarmed in their heads as in a market. Thoughts jabbered, weighed down and jostled each other. Shame cast a veil across their eyes. They had to get as far away as possible from Papa Archibald, who had warned them of love's torment. Never ever to meet his gaze again. They went up and came down hills unknown to them. They made their way night and day, in sunlight and in moonlight, paired just as they were. They crossed rivers and strode through canefields which pointed their blooms, identical to a thousand war arrows, to the heavens. They ended up in a land with no memory. There they were taken on as servants. They revealed to no one their condition and consecrated the lie by saying that they had no family. They both gave birth on the same day, within two hours of each other, to Myrtha and Mirna. The little girls were born almost as twins too, similar in every way. The sisters made their home in a cabin behind God's back, but the babies really thrived, suckling the milk of life. A month went by. And then a fever took hold of one of the babies who succumbed in an attack, at that very moment, in the bath water. Was it Mirna or Myrtha?

'It's your Myrtha!' screamed the young Barnabé.

'No! I recognised her by the birthmark she has on her bottom, it is your Mirna who is lying there!' declared Boniface.

'That is your little one lying in this coffin of white wood!' asserted Barnabé, dragging from her sister's arms the living infant.

'Give her back to me! You are mistaken, your Mirna is dead! Give me my daughter!' wailed Boniface, grabbing back the child.

Then they drew lots. And fate, that scoundrel, decided that Mirna should take the short road to heaven. Her daughter buried, Barnabé had nothing left to care for, not even a little tame dog to caress. Thenceforth, her life lost all meaning. Already she was haunted, as if Satan was prodding her, by the sins absolved by the birth of her Mirna. By dying, the beloved child took with her the kite of hope to which Barnabé had clung up to then. In spite of everything the two sisters were reconciled with each other. And the days once more passed sadly. But far, very far from the ears of her twin, the poor mother called the surviving girl by the first name of the dead child...

'Mirna, my pretty one, my everything, my beloved!'

One day, a big Congo Negro presented himself before them. He was named Mérinés. He wanted to set up house with Boni. He accepted the little girl, swore that he would be a good father, swore before God. Boniface left one fine Sunday during the rainy season, to see the country, on the arm of this idiot, poor as Job, who had nothing to offer a woman besides sharing the little he had to eat and his unbounded, useless love. Myrtha was almost two years old. The sisters kissed each other. 'Say goodbye to Aunt Baba! Yes, you will see her, every Sunday! After all, Guadeloupe is not that big!' They laughed, giving each other little jealous, grudging kisses.

Suddenly, old Barnabé fell silent, as if she just heard something whispered by the wind. She raised her head. A band of black clouds was choking the sun's light. A moment went by before she added, in an undertone, wiping a tear away:

'She was seventeen years, when I saw her again the next time, my Mirna...For fifteen years Boniface hid her from me. She did not stay in one place with her Mérinés. They were always on the move so that I could not find them. I scoured all of Guadeloupe. Believe me...'

But I see from your eyes that you want to know the reason behind the old woman's confidences. Well, I learned later that her head had taken off to the land where square is round and fish fly. She took each young girl for her one and only Mirna and related her life story to all those women who had time for her.

VI
A Burial in Exchange for Cloves of Passion

Boniface's burial did not stir up too many Christian folk. The cortège was strung out thinly like a young skinny pig. All alone in the world, at the head of the procession, Mérinés miserably dragged his body along the way to the cemetery. Since Boni had left him behind, he no longer spoke to anyone. Not even to

Myrtha, who walked behind him, head high, shoulders squared, dressed all in black. Then followed the future in-laws, in full force: Ma Ninette, who was crying as if Boniface had been her actual sister; Sosthène, invoking Jesus Christ to keep his eyes in front of him as they constantly drifted towards Myrtha's rounded behind; Léonce, a worthy fiancé, wearing a crêpe armband; Hector, meditating on the fleeting nature of life and the certainty of death; Lucina, dreaming of leaving as soon as possible the imbeciles of Haute-Terre. At the rear, a few neighbours, all smiles, who had come to fill out the the procession. But in truth, another spectacle captured the attention of the curious onlookers: a woman walking close to the cortège. She was wearing a loose dress of brownish satin gathered at the waist by a wide wine-coloured belt and, shading her face, a massive black hat with a veil. As she went by, the people elbowed each other, moved away, whispered, grumbled indignantly and made the sign of the cross while trembling. Perhaps it was not a lie after all...Ma Boniface must have dealt with the souls of the damned and frequented spirits that could fly.

After the funeral, Mérinés, alone and paralysed by grief, no longer opened his door to anyone. They say, however, that he received one visit after this sad day. Rumours spread about the man. Folks in the neighbourhood were on the lookout, telling stories that he was not as alone as all that in his mashed-up cabin. They often encountered words that had slipped out through the door, running madly into the road.

Once (he still remembers it today even though he is wrinkled and losing his mind a little) a young fellow, Annibal by name – perhaps more curious than the rest – wanted to pay a so-called visit to the widower. Imagine his astonishment when he heard a woman's voice tearing to pieces all that was going on, in this case the muffled grumblings of brother Mérinés. Ah! Ah! Ah! thought the boy, the widower is no friend of solitude! A new sweetie is already installed, the old rascal! Annibal turned around immediately, in a hurry to spread throughout the town the news of this recovery. But he had not gone more than a few paces when he felt behind him the rasping creak of a door being opened. He spun around, the smile of a real idiot already spreading across his black lips. A shiver went down his spine. The sight was unbearable. His stomach became heavy and stiff like three tons of cement hardened in the bag because of rain. He saw death before him...In flesh and bone! The dead woman, buried two moons earlier, looked him up and down with evil intent. Ma Boniface alive! Our visitor, suddenly weak-kneed because of the otherworldly vision, drew on all his strength, raised one leg, then the other, repeated the manoeuvre two-three times. Finally, momentum built up. He ran, quickly, robust athlete in the fading light. He made the sign of the cross. And continued to run, the forest an accomplice in his flight. When he got to town, his tongue was loosened. Boniface tried to block his path. He related how he faced her down, brandishing the cross hanging from his neck. It seemed the devil woman backed away. Fire blazed from her ears and her mouth spewed out animals. Naturally, they believed his every word, thinking that Mérinés was a great obeahman and that the dead woman had turned into a zombie to practise magic.

For quite a while, long after the widower disappeared without saying farewell, many were those who came face to face with Boniface. She appeared everywhere. On the banks of rivers, at the edge of the forest, on leaving parties, they whispered her name while hurriedly making the sign of the cross and saying 'Ave Maria's. For many decades, nightfall surprised only the brave on lonely roads. Everyone came home early. Doors and windows were shut to ward off the sounds of the dark, both strange and familiar, while the shadows lengthened in the lamplight. Their heads hidden under sheets, children trembled on their pallets and kept silent. They all knew that Ma Boniface was on the prowl until after midnight and would carry them off if they were not as well behaved as the sacred images stuck up on the walls of the cabin...Yes, Boniface, poor innocent woman, bundle of bones in the cemetery ground, must have wondered what madness took hold of the people of Haute-Terre, who mixed her name up with all this satanic mishmash. Did those people not know that she had an identical twin named Barnabé?

Of course, it was the sister the Congo fellow had found outside the door. The same one who shocked everyone with her red belt. The same one who caused that animal Annibal to bolt. When Mérinés saw her, a wintry chill blew down his spine. She raised her veil. He almost fell over backward and crossed himself. Had his Boni come back to life? He squinted so as to sharpen his view. On that day, the moon was not full. The rainy season was approaching. At this time, the sun left its place in the sky early. No, he would not retreat. A courageous man, he had the spirit of an old fighting cock at its last fight. Fearlessly he advanced. He called three times: 'Boni! Oh, Boni! Is it you, Boni?' And his voice, tiny and weak at the outset, strengthened as he walked on. Suddenly, he understood. 'Barnabé! You came, my sister!' The twin sister did not open her mouth, nodded her head and, stepping past him, went into the house as if it was hers.

Myrtha went down the hill with her infernal bucket of water. Once again, Léonce cursed the mayor, who had taken note of his request but made no move to bring water up to his house. Léonce jumped up and down but only the privileged few had running water at that time. Seeing her like this, going up and down the hillside, exposed to the gaze of the fellows in town, he was not a happy chap. He considered his Myrtha a queen and now cursed this bucket of water which his young wife wore like a crown of misery, making her walk humpbacked as she made her way up the hill. He cursed his luck and resented the mayor, his assistants and all the scamps who ogled Myrtha's sit-upon. He wanted them to respect her...alas, each day she had to go down to the town to face the rascals' leers.

The young woman, unlike Léonce, was not particularly distressed by this task. The quest for drinking water — awkward though it might be — was not the heart of her existence. A rare beauty and a man poorly served by the joys of the flesh sometimes form a pair of souls well suited to each other. Myrtha finally saw her dream being fulfilled and everything made her happy. It must be said, without being modest, that Léonce overwhelmed her. Myrtha melted more quickly than sorbet when she snuggled up to that powerful chest. The sweetest of husbands, a coconut sweetie, he was, like the pleasing taste of eggnog on 1 January and a poet...all heart...What more can you ask of the Lord?

Myrtha's flower, the bud of a poppy clenched tight like a fist, bloomed painlessly during their wedding night. When they awoke next morning, a purple orchid nestled in the soft bed. Myrtha's deflowering brought her no grief. On the contrary, she kept on laughing while scrubbing vigorously this dried flower which sealed, better than the ink on the marriage certificate, her union with Léonce.

The newlyweds rose with the dawn, shortly after the cocks had sounded their clarion call. For a moment they considered the firmness of the beams that sheltered their love and left, right there on the warm bed, their bodies hot with the night. Quickly, habits became fixed, each one marked out their territory. On mornings, Myrtha never ventured a word without first cleaning her teeth and rinsing out her mouth with water. Léonce was calm before the silence of this dawn, the wide-eyed gaze she directed at him, the rustle of fabric and the squeaking of the floorboards which filled his heart with a flood of questions, where evil, self-doubt and regret fought each other with bare fists. In keeping with her, he no longer spoke, but lived these early wordless mornings like the end of the world. To rid himself of his fears and to ward off ill-luck, he took his Bible, which always lay open on the dresser, then lit a taper. Ma Ninette had assured him that this procedure would purify the air and chase away evil spirits that people kept seeing above Haute-Terre. He knelt down and, totally absorbed, he pursued his reading of the Scriptures, an engrossing serial that he had read four or five times. After cleaning her teeth, Myrtha half-opened the door and immediately began to talk, breathlessly, bouncing on the bed all the while. 'Tell me, honey! Are you going to plant sweet potatoes today? Ah! You should weed the bed of chives this morning! And what do you think of these banana suckers that Eurose brought you, rainbow figs you think? I should have two-three cents for the shop. We need salt and there is no more oil either! What am I to put on the fire this midday? Fish or beef...I should go to the seaside. You like cod, if you want some, so do I...'

As soon as he heard this refrain, Léonce once more came to life and closed his Bible with the small smile of the reborn. He rose clumsily, left the book wide open in its place, blew out the candle and left the room. In the kitchen, he pulled up a chair and, seating himself, gave his reply:

'Warm the coffee, Myrtha!' No, he did not bark at her. He spoke without raising his voice but with just the right authority that his new status as a married man conferred on him. His wife obeyed, twirling around him, like a moth lost in the dawn's light. She undressed and washed her privates, talking all the while. While he sipped the strong brew, she busied herself plaiting and unplaiting her hair, asking him a thousand questions. After dressing herself, she opened wide doors and windows. With a gush, fresh air rushed into the cabin. At that moment, revived by the frugal meal, Léonce felt rising within him quite a different hunger excited by the scent of Myrtha. But the garden awaited him. Outside, life exploded, with all the passion of a young bride-to-be. His hat askew on his head, his loins girded by a thick cord, he studied the mood of the sky, picked up his machete and off he went, barefoot, a fullness in his heart. Unlike the fellows in the area, Léonce took care of his garden alone. You are a man! he would say to himself. Try to show it and bring back enough of what is needed to keep your wife happy!

Myrtha's days all began with the inevitable trek for water at the pipe in town. Even though Léonce had placed, in two locations in the cabin and on the roof, large sheets of curved zinc to channel the water from the heavens into drums, she could not escape this burdensome duty. Despite the warnings of the doctor-mayor, who continued to repeat: 'Give up this practice, your children will not survive! There are several pipes here and there. Go find drinking water!' whole families continued to drink water from the barrels, without fear of illness. Myrtha had much to do in the house. But, after the departure of Léonce and before getting down to her chores, she slumped into a chair, stretched her legs wide before her and, limp like a person after a long trip, she considered her lot, made plans and dreamed of the future. All was going well. Léonce planted and reaped. The hens and the roosters grew in number. The rabbits were sold by the dozen in the market; the hutch was never empty. The pigs wallowed heavily in their sty; at Christmas, Léonce planned to slaughter three. And the cabin, standing tall without prop or patch, sheltered the happiness of her union with a cripple who had no evil in him. So, picture her thrill in going down the hill and showing off to the town folk, eager to see domestic disputes, her carefree, joyful state – even if the return turned out to be less glorious. About seven o'clock, she spread her sheets out in the sun, beat the mattress, swept the house and went off to empty the chamberpot in the river. Then, she prepared a meal for her Léonce: a chunk of bread, avocado and cucumber when in season, biscuits, fritters...Around ten o'clock, he always sat at the foot of a huge star-apple tree that he had found there, spreading its welcome shade. He took off his hat to better size up the task he had completed and mopped his brow with the chequered kerchief that was tied around his neck. While waiting for Myrtha, he often thought of the first time she set foot on these hills and placed her hand on his heart. He did not quite believe his good fortune, so he shook his head left and right to shake off this crazy dream. He took some earth in his hands, pulled up some tufts of grass, in order to reassure himself that he was really and truly married to the most beautiful woman in the world. Suddenly, he was jubilant, straightened his shoulders and, as if by a miracle, the young bride appeared, carrying a basket under her arm.

They ate in silence, side by side. And then the final mouthfuls suddenly made remote the projects that once made them agitated. Arms pointed here and there. Eyes already saw the extent of their prosperity. When the basket had nothing left to offer, they rose together. Nothing left to say, they felt ill at ease suddenly, felt they were strangers and ran off each in a separate direction, disturbed by having confided so much to each other, panic-stricken at the words they dared to utter and the pitfalls of happiness. Léonce left the garden three hours after midday. In order to find his way back to Myrtha, he had only to follow the smell of the lunch that wafted over to him. Myrtha lay claim to being a famous cook. Her gravies, soups, stews and curries deserved medals and awards. She put in each of her creations the flavour of love, a few pinches of tenderness and cloves of passion which he wiped from his dish with his eyes closed. What more can a man ask of the Lord? A child! he said to himself, holding out his plate for a refill.

VII
The Nut and the Seeds

Ma Ninette often visited the young couple. Because of his deformity, she was particularly fond of Léonce. She missed him so much now. Everyone knew she had arranged the marriage in spite of herself. She did not like the girl that much. Myrtha remained in her view a little black female with no redeeming quality who deserved neither fuss nor fanfare. In the church, when she saw Léonce hand her the gold ring, her heart contracted suddenly while her knees trembled in her stockings of khaki-coloured cotton. Well before the marriage, a self-righteous few advised her not to succumb to the spirit of festivity, given the fact that the bride-to-be was recently in mourning and that the good Lord would take a dim view of the living having a good time. She was told that people would go crazy dancing so close to a mother's coffin. Ninette scoffed at these words of advice. She preferred to run the risk of divine wrath than to deprive her son of a proper marriage. She nevertheless took her precautions, recited three 'Pater Noster's, deposited an offering in each collection box in the church and knelt until Christ in person urged her to advance the date of the ceremony and to pay no heed to the period of mourning.

Between us, you must realise that there was some urgency about the marriage. It was six months since Ma Boniface ceased an upright existence and was rotting in the poisoned belly of the burial ground. Three months since father Mérinés had left Haute-Terre; he was said to have gone off with a *femme fatale*. Six months since Myrtha had been living under the family's roof. Ninette felt it was like six centuries while Sosthène – you remember his weakness for women! – devoured the beautiful girl with his eyes. He prayed to resist the temptation which governed his feelings, but could not suppress the surges of his pointed blade, always ready to strike, that was clenched between his legs. Six months of Ninette guarding Myrtha's chastity. She was bone weary. She crumpled into a chair, frazzled, nightmares assailed every pore in her skin. She tossed about, wept, sweated and begged whenever she put down her head. And the too-well-oiled wheels of her imagination began to spin wildly. 'Good God, no! Sosthène, don't sow your seed in her!' she screamed, choking. 'Jesus! Have mercy, Sosthène, keep her free from your juice! My God, spare me!' The poor woman awoke in a trance, baffled, no longer knowing whether she was still dreaming or whether, in truth, her old husband rose and fell between the girl's thighs, fondled her bottom, suckled her pum pum and dragged at her breasts. Suddenly, she leaped out of the chair, her eye-lashes flickered and she opened her mouth wide to give vent to her horror. But, deep in her throat, her screams remained frozen. Sosthène was right there, as well behaved as one of the wise men, sitting legs together, reading his Bible like a good boy.

They could have lived comfortably in the house. Myrtha slept in Lucina's bedroom. Léonce shared the adjoining room with his brother Hector. And Ninette, poor and powerless, despite her advancing years and without any desire, spent her nights having to contend with Sosthène's tool and his seeds. She sought some-how to satisfy him, saying to herself that a full belly does not covet the neighbour's lunch. No, Ninette did not laugh when the old goat mounted her wrinkled belly, squealing, 'Ay! Ay! Ay! Ninette...' She knew that what was really going through his head even more loudly was, 'Ay! Ay! Ay! Myrtha...' Mercifully, he did not take long and soon fell asleep after satisfying himself. Nevertheless, Ninette kept one eye open. She did not allow herself to be taken in by Sosthène's snores and stayed on the alert all night. Just in case she slipped into sleep, the poor woman contrived to hang on to an arm, a leg or a piece of clothing from the old scamp. Better to be safe than sorry, she kept telling herself, waking from a sleep riven by nightmares. Sometimes, in the middle of the night, Sosthène tried to extricate himself in order to urinate. Ninette's grip automatically tightened, like the pincers of a hairy crab.

'Is just a pee I want to take, dear! Pee, just pee, Ninette!' The bed creaked. Sosthène got up. Ninette sat at the edge of the bed, and they both listened dutifully to the spray crashing into the chamberpot.

The marriage therefore became a matter of life and death. If things continued like this, Ninette would end up in the cemetery before Christmas, chatting away with Ma Boniface. Mourning or no mourning, she had to remove far from Sosthène's eyes and nose this unopened flower with its overwhelming scent. We have been unkind in talking about Ninette, but at least she clung to her pride. She could no longer keep track of the women deflowered by her husband, the bastards he fathered at every corner and the innumerable blows to her honour, but her sense of morality could not tolerate such an affront. Sosthène opening the pathway before Léonce. Sosthène of the unclean juice driving his seed into Myrtha's belly. Sosthène buried in his Bible after it was too late...Léonce would not have survived. If Ninette had not dragged him back on to the bank of hope, resuscitated him as it were, he would have succumbed to his love for this little black girl. No, Léonce did not deserve any such indignity. A blow of this enormity would have shattered his existence.

'Six months of mourning! You have done your duty, Myrtha! Time passes quickly for us poor sinners on God's earth. Do not put off this marriage any longer! Jesus Christ has even give me permission already. Where misfortune has cast her, your mother does not have half of the worries that plague my mind. If you only knew...Come on, believe me, it is time! Look before you! If you focus your eyes a little, you will see a fine young person and a new cabin standing on a hill. They await you. What will happen to both of you, no one can predict. Today, your hearts beat with the same rhythm...but who can say for how long?'

The following week, the banns were published. And, exactly seven months after the burial of Boniface, the town of Haute-Terre, in full force, danced in the ceremonial room of the town hall. The day after the marriage, Ninette succumbed to a great torpor which lasted a full three months. But her heart was lighter, with relief. She had saved the young couple from being exposed to Sosthène's insatiable appetite. At least no one could say that she had captured the flesh of a young chicken and then served it for her old rooster to feed on! Or even worse, that

Léonce was some kind of bloody fool who plants, waters, weeds, clears and then falls asleep, allowing thieves to eat and reap.

Since the departure of the newly married couple, Ninette slept much better. The obligations of the marriage taken care of, she fell into a deep sleep. Sosthène then quickly reverted to his old pre-Myrtha habits. One escaped for every hundred that lined up. After his daughter-in-law's departure, he immediately came back to his senses and deserted the house. He roamed far and wide. The enraptured chicks lay down, opened up to and loved him, for as long as the illusion lasted. Alas, there was the other side of the coin. He always rose wild-eyed after his transgression. And he fled, distraught, silent, at top speed from this phenomenal womanising, which was not his true nature. As for the females, they awakened from the nightmare, and, realising that it was too late, they hurled curses whistling like blank shots which hit him in the back and...

I know, even if you are not interested in your neighbour's business, you by now must be asking yourself how this perpetual philanderer could have chosen of all women the uninteresting haunches and ordinary ring-finger of Ninette. Sosthène often thought of the strange circumstance that led him, bovinely, before the pockmarked face of the mayor all trussed up in his tricolour ribbon and then stammering before the priest. He could not say what made him offer up an I DO to Étiennette, this I DO

62

that blasphemed fidelity. When he thought of it, he glimpsed the Devil at work, tail flying, horns and hooves gleaming, stoking around him – Sosthène, miserable sinner! – the flames of hell…Since his extended youth, a simple wink would overwhelm the chicks. All of them! Like flies! He picked them up one by one without haste and laced them with the juice from his belly bottom. One day, he saw a girl disembarking with a solid backside and firm bubbies. They said that on the leeward side, her mother practised obeah. Her fisherman father had fallen for a chick from Haute-Terre who sewed for a living. The man spent his time equally between these two women. He passionately loved the seamstress, but the obeahwoman pulled the strings that held him tight. He struggled to resist the temptation of the flesh which enslaved him at the feet of the beauty of Haute-Terre. Alas!…The latter consulted a fixer-man who was capable of doing great harm. Etiennette often accompanied her father. They would spend three days, sometimes a week there. The seamstress made dresses for Ninette in order to buy her silence and complicity. And the girl paraded in the main street, draped in silk and a reputation for chastity. When Sosthène saw her, he gave her the usual look. Normally, the young women would change course at that very instant, follow him, sleep with him and so on…No one knew the whys or wherefores, but Étiennette was like marble. Cold! Colder than the massive funeral slab which covered over three generations of the deceased Cassidy de Bouze, a family of white Creoles, the offspring of cold, slave-owning ancestors. Could the blood flowing in the veins of those whites be warm? Are the veins running through marble icy cold? Questions crowded the young Sosthène's mind. Previously, it was said that he had taken half of the eligible women in Guadeloupe. He had never come up against marble. Is it true that marble does not have a crack...not even a tiny split to slip in the little finger? How to penetrate this great mystery? For a moment, he imagined that Étiennette, female with an enchanting backside – because it was beyond his reach – did not have, squeezed between her thighs, that accommodating, sweet-smelling, moist and warm treat...that slit common to all women, that opening that has powers of life and death over men!...Sosthène caught himself. No! Far from it, a fire must be blazing under this skirt, he decided, guessing wildly. He looked around him and saw no one who could deserve Ninette. Only he had claims to this trophy. You want politeness, how about flowers! The French language thrown across her path. Ninette did not bend. Pure marble! All Sosthène's machinations were shattered by this icon of purity. Charm did not work. That is how, dazed and stammering, he landed up in the town hall and the church. And that is how those two, who had nothing in common, found themselves joined in the sight of God and man. Ninette was not brimming with passion. During their wedding night, she glowed as much as a soaked candle.

64

Nevertheless, Sosthène did his business. But he learned, a little late, that solid backsides and proud bearings sometimes conceal caverns where the sun does not shine. The following day, he returned to the country roads that he knew so well and left Ninette weeping in the cabin.

In the year that Léonce got married, Sosthène turned fifty. He prayed as much as he sinned, not knowing when death would put down its baggage in front of his door. Each day, he asked the Lord to cast out of his body the evil spirit that corrupted his life. Ninette did not give a damn about his roving, about his determination to escape his curse, about his endless praying; she gave it up in the sheets. Her life with him was a real mess but she stayed put, taking her iron, because she had said yes to the shackles of marriage. Despite the example of a scoundrel's existence led by their father, she persisted in giving a Christian education to her children. On that day, she entered her forties. To your way of thinking, what could a woman hope for at this time, when the bell tolled this age for her to hear?... When the spouse was an animal like Sosthène and when the eldest boy had left home to try out married life? Tell me! What could a woman of that age, prematurely grey from destiny's telling blows, expect from the rest of her existence on her feet?... Mere flesh! Born of flesh, because she was dust, she would return to dust. That's why she climbed the hill so eagerly in order to question the girl each day. Alas, it was nine months since the consummation of the marriage. And nothing. Myrtha's belly was a moon swept by the winds of suffering and promises never kept.

That morning, the shadows of misfortune and doom crowded the thoughts of Ninette. She said to herself, with his bad luck, Léonce must have picked up the curse of sterility. Perhaps Myrtha had a spell cast on her…Satan's disciples, the accursed and the obeahmen made their filthy money from spoiling women's eggs, ruining businesses and murdering the innocent. As for jealousy, it sailed like a transatlantic steamer right down the middle of the main street of the town. And so it was, all the flotsam and jetsam swept down by her thoughts bumped against each other in Ninette's brain box, just like vicious crabs left to drain in the black insides of barrels before Easter.

VIII
The Ways of Chance

In 1963, I had completed three years as a struggling student in Paris. Each academic year found me in a new discipline. I first strode along the path of literature but Latin threw me off the track. For a while history caught my eye, just ahead of political science, with the future of the country in mind, you never know. My schoolteacher mother was full of complaints concerning my delinquency and sent me letters elaborating on her hopes, prayers and all the dreams she built around me. My father begged me to find the way to success which he said was lined with university diplomas. I did not have my heart in my studies. To slave away alone, a prisoner of the four walls of my maid's room, drove me to despair. I thought of the servants who had been through there, weeping with loneliness, or ravaged by some marquis, swallowing poison, suffocating a child. I thought I heard them sighing. I felt like dying. In the month of August a steamer took me back to Guadeloupe. I was not returning with the ghost of a certificate. I had had enough of the Faculty and the students. What would I say to them this time? I had to find something solid . . . a calling! The third day of the crossing, photography occurred to me like a flash of inspiration.

'Spoil a future which was so promising!' moaned my father.

'And if you were to try the Training College!' suggested my mother.

'If you really applied yourself . . . photography is no career for you! You should register for English. That is nice, teacher of English! What do you say to that?' suggested my uncle Alfred.

'Photography, a thankless profession!' Great-aunt Isora assured me.

Mercifully I was my parents' only child and my wishes were commands they hastened to execute. Two days after the declaration of my new vocation, I found on my bed a brand-new camera and a series of addresses for schools in Paris ready to receive me with open arms. That very afternoon, my mother dug up the photos of my cabins from the Caribbean. Instantly, I remembered old Barnabé. I had not thought about her for three full years. I immediately felt like seeing her again, for her to tell me one last time about her tormented youth or, who knows, reveal to me even more disturbing secrets...

It has been said often enough, curiosity sometimes takes you along the pathways of chance where logic and reason get lost in the twists and turns of the hills and sprout at the edge of crazy rivers. All my thoughts rushed towards her. I had to take a picture of her, to remember her, before she was dead and her cabin demolished.

'I was expecting you, Mirna. God be praised, you have come! Every day I prayed to the Almighty: You who sees all, who knows all, who hears every thought... guide her steps towards me! Make me touch her one last time before returning to that state of dust of which we know the cause. This is how I said it: Lord! Grant me this favour so that, my heart happy, I can close my eyes at last.'

More battered than an old coffee pot wheezing and puffing on an antiquated stove, the sorry creature opened her arms to me. She was rocking in the middle of the room, completely draped in a spider's web. The narrow, shaky rocker moved around the floor creaking cra cra cra...

'Come in, so come in, Mirna! Don't be afraid, you

are at home here, this is your inheritance! God be praised you came in time! You know death will come for me in three days, at the very moment the Devil marries his daughter behind the church and rain and sun begin to chatter right in the heart of the sky...'

I wanted to back away, to behave like those wicked spirits who play hide and seek with the living. But the power of the crazy words pushed me on the contrary towards this old abandoned mother. Butts of Job cigarettes littered the ground. The room stank of stale tobacco and, in the corners, melted candle wax made white stains on the dirty floor.

'Three days, Mirna... Just three days and then it is all over. Don't cry, come on. I will go without suffering. God be praised! So approach, come closer! Come on, repeat after me: I am Mirna, the one and only daughter of Barnabé! Say it one more time... My mother is called Barnabé and my name is Mirna. Louder! Mirna, Mirna, Mirna! Now, give me a little kiss! Tell me, how is your family? Your last one and your twins give you plenty trouble, eh! And your husband, tell me... Aha! You did not know that I knew your people! Think, concentrate a little. Have you never seen a person in a veil hanging around your house? You didn't notice me in my black dress at Boniface's funeral? I had put on a red belt for you... For you to realise that you had not become a poor orphan.'

I knew nothing of Mirna's life. Hadn't the old woman dreamed up this husband, these children, this carnival of a funeral? I quite liked the poor creature and it pained

me to see her pulling on the string of misery. When I
moved forward to give her the kiss she was waiting for,
she began to cry. Small yellowish tears, like dirty water.
And her voice, ruined by tobacco, broke into this
lament:

> 'The little boy of mine
> Asked for the breast
> I gave him
> The breast to eat
> Sleep little one
> Daddy not there
> Is Mamma one
> In one big trouble
> Sleep little one
> Daddy not there
> Is Mamma one
> In grief...'

She suddenly fell silent, dried her tears and her eyes
drifted back to the past.

'You remember that song, eh! You didn't even have
teeth when I sang it to you, and yet you were
laughing, you already understood.'

She resumed singing. Softly, even more softly...

> 'Is Mamma all alone
> In grief
> Sleep little one
> Daddy not there
> Is Mamma one...'

'But why were you hiding like that? I asked her. 'Why all the silence?'

She raised her eyes, placed a trembling hand on my head, then began to fondle my hair, nervously, shyly, like a young mother who, for the first time, feels her child's flesh.

'I had nothing to offer you, Mirna. I let you leave with your aunt. The wicked woman hid you from me! She stole you! She wanted you for herself alone. After ten years, I swore to the good Lord to no longer get mixed up in her life, to no longer walk behind her all over Guadeloupe...to behave as though I never had a twin, as if I never had Mirna...One day, fate made me cross your path in La Pointe. You were not yet sixteen. That's when I learned that you were staying in Haute-Terre. It was already too late. What could I have said? Would you have believed my version of the truth? After Boniface's death, I thought of taking you away with me...but you got engaged to this cripple. I went to see that mule, the scoundrel Mérinés, the one who never begat you nor raised you. He told me rubbish about you poisoning your poor mother. I replied: "It was written. Boni took what was destined for me, she must pay for my sorrow!" He said to me: "You've lost your little girl! Her heart is hard and she likes money only! She is going to get married just to get the cabin sitting on the hill that you saw on your way here." That's when I realised that the time for reunions was past. I made my way back. But I always returned, as if a thorn was in my side. Sometimes, you saw me in the distance. You called to me. I hid my face and disappeared. Tell me, now that you are here, so close to your mamma...tell me, did you really marry Léonce because of his cabin? Now that your children are grown and your life has no tomorrow...tell me, would you not have cursed your mother, if she had appeared before you, the time when, sitting in your house chatting to yourself, you thought that, perhaps, if you had been given the name you were born with, you would have had a different future, have fared better...

> 'Sleep little one
> Daddy not there
> Is Mamma one
> Who is in grief
> Little one sleep...'

IX
An Extraordinary Garden

That morning, it is possible Ninette showed Myrtha how to spread her thighs and raise her legs in order to allow her boy's sperm to go more deeply into her body. It is quite probable that, on returning to town, she put this thorny problem in the hands of a fixer-man in order to shed some light on that moonless night through which she wandered ever since she suspected that the girl was a tormented soul. Perhaps she consulted some old woman with children who had a secret stock of magic leaves and remedies that worked. However, what is certain is that as a good God-fearing Christian woman, she confided her sorrow to the Lord and placed her hopes for the future at the feet of the Lamb of God. Whatever the case, the following month Myrtha did not need to take out her period cloths. Her breasts grew swollen and her belly round like a young calabash. Ninette said nothing about it to anyone but, from this moment, she became deeply convinced that she alone was the reason for this miracle. Sometimes she heard words from the other world. She felt a hand on her shoulder and saw shadows turning around her. She said to herself that a little of her mother's magic powers had come down to her without her noticing.

Léonce knew, because of his wisdom, that you do not foolishly rejoice at the egg stuck in the hen's belly before it is hatched. He maintained his restraint, but deep in his guts, he was torn by wild bursts of emotion. For many moons now a bout of diarrhoea left him like wrung-out clothes. For days constipation left him swollen all over. Sun up sun down, a hiccup so upset him that he felt he was at death's door. Sometimes he fell into a bottomless ditch and, in the middle of his field, he stumbled and, half drunk with happiness and fear mixed together, staggered, dazed, into a star-apple tree. Sometimes, even, the stubborn seed which entered Myrtha's belly purely and simply erased his own birth defect. Truly, he looked in vain at his disturbing limb from all angles, he could see only harmony and perfection. It was in the time of great transformations that his gift came back to him. He himself had forgotten he was born with a caul.

...Ma Octavia, Sosthène's mother, died at the age of seventy and a bit. She roundly cursed her daughter-in-law when she found her pounding the caul:

'So, are you blind, Ninette! You listen to the crap from this philanderer, Sosthène, who is good for nothing better than seducing women! You are blind, but your son will see further than you! You weep because he has a club-foot...and you wish to take his gift away from him! So you do not see that his club-foot is the fulfilment of this blessing!' Octavia hated Ninette, whom she called the big-ass girl. She did not understand this marriage and assumed that Ninette must be worth her weight in evil spells, in order to become Missus before church and state. However, Sosthène was her only child and so she gave him a half of her yard on which to build a house. They lived like tongue and teeth on this little stretch of land. Nothing that came into Ninette's house escaped Octavia's ears. The wind bore all that was said, but Octavia did not get involved. She left the doomed couple to themselves. Because of this business with the caul, for a whole decade, Octavia no longer greeted either Sosthène or Ninette. If need be, she called the pickney, who came running immediately, because the problems of older folk did not concern little children...One day, she did not open her door. Come evening, Sosthène urged on Léonce, because he quite loved his mamma and was worried about her health. The boy found his grandmamma across her bed, frothing like cow's-foot soup, her mouth twisted, the right side stiffer than a regiment standing at attention.

Ma Octavia knew she was susceptible to strokes. Her head was blazing hot. Her vision blurred. Her hand became numb. And she said that colonies of ants were marching across her old body. She knew only her own remedies. Without further ado, she went off to open two-three passion fruits, drank off the juice, chewed a clove of garlic and, bravely, her hoe on her shoulder, returned to the garden. Her sin was too much salt in her food. When she fell ill, her pride took a beating; she peed and shat on herself. Like a dutiful daughter, Ninette took care of her as if it were her own mother. Without hearing the slightest word of thanks in return, she bathed her, fixed her hair, fed her three times a day and hauled every morning her soiled clothes off to the river for washing. That is how Ninette lost her last child, undone by her natural goodness. She remained in bed as long as was necessary to mourn her loss and to heap curses on the cruel woman who made her see so much misery.

If Léonce hadn't taken care of her, his grandmother would have been dead the rainy season of that same year. Besides himself, no one paid attention to her. He visited her each morning before school, cleaned her up, then made her swallow puréed breadfruit, which the sick old woman spat back out, swearing all the while. Every day Ninette shouted from her window:

'Leave her be! She will kill you, son! That woman is an old witch! Make her dead!'

Léonce did not budge. Two years went by like this. One morning, towards the end, at a time when she hardly spoke any more, except with rasping and grumbling, she grabbed the hand of the little lame boy and whispered to him this strange prediction:

'You know that your grandmother will soon die...yes, yes, like everyone else down here! Listen closely! I will change how I look the day I die. You see me ugly and twisted up today, but soon I will become a beautiful young girl. Listen! Before the first grey hairs sprout from your head, we will find each other again...I will come to see you and you will not be afraid to speak to me...because you have the gift!'

The child was not afraid. He immediately opened his eyes and mouth in order to get a better look at his grandmother. Alas, her white hair, which had never known the touch of a comb, stood up like a mangrove. From her twisted mouth seeped a yellowish drivel that had to be wiped every second. And in her flared nostrils, twin caverns were home to a dark world of white hairs and old, dried-up snot.

'Do not be afraid!' Octavia said to him. 'On my last day, I will not look like that!'

When she died, in the burning heat of the dry

season of the year 1923, Léonce was alone with her. That morning, for the first time, she had not soiled her sheets and smiled in her bed as the boy entered. She was neither hungry nor thirsty and wanted only one thing: for him to read her a verse chosen at random from the Bible. A kind of agitation had taken hold of her. This is what the reading turned out to be:

'They shall confess their iniquity, and the iniquity of their fathers, with their trespass which they trespassed against me, and that they have walked contrary unto me, and that I also have walked contrary unto them and have brought them into the land of their enemies. And then their uncircumcised hearts will be humbled and they will accept the punishment of their iniquity. Then I will remember my covenant with Jacob, and also my covenant with Isaac and also my covenant with Abraham and I will remember the land. The land also shall be left of them and shall enjoy her sabbaths while she lieth desolate without them; and they shall accept of the punishment of their iniquity, because they despised my judgements and because their soul abhorred my statutes...'

When Octavia raised her good hand, Léonce fell silent. It had all been said. She forced a smile for the child, who, at that time, had no knowledge of the gentlemen Isaac, Jacob and Abraham. And then, she murmured:'Don't forget, Léonce! Don't forget to look at my face in preparation for the day we meet again!'

Then, while she breathed her last breath, Léonce saw the old wrinkled skin stretched smooth miraculously. All the folds disappeared and her mouth righted itself like a canoe on a calm sea. In his granny's bed there now lay a young girl unmarked by the years, a beautiful black woman with a complexion like a naseberry and a white head of hair.

The gift came back...perhaps because of the seed that grew in Myrtha's belly. Perhaps because Léonce's mind was topsy-turvy. One thing was certain, it was this same young girl with white hair who, in his garden, far from the inquisitive and from old zombies, appeared to Léonce. He had fallen into a short sleep at the foot of the star-apple tree. He had hardly fallen asleep when he awoke. A completely different person. As if he was emerging from his body to be born a second time. A very fine film veiled his eyes. A song of joy rose to his lips, for a miracle had happened. Around him the garden that he had left without a trace of fruit was bursting with fruitfulness. The branches of the avocado tree sagged under the weight of their produce. The red peppers, in abundance, exploded under the leaves. Mandarins, oranges, grapefruits, glowing by the thousand from each branch, spread their aroma across the hillside. The sprouting cane looked like a giant sea urchin, so dense were the innumerable, bristling shoots, as if their points were ready to pierce the heavens. The three banana trees that he loved had produced phenomenal bunches which, judging by their appearance, each weighed more than a ton. And then he came to a halt before the breadfruit tree. The puny shoot, planted the previous month, dominated everything, standing some thirty feet tall. In its branches, laden with breadfruit, nestled colourful and glittering fauna: Sapho comet birds, macaws with blue and yellow feathers, topaz hummingbirds, puffins, pigeons, red flamingos, parakeets, blackbirds, lovebirds, frigate birds, parrots with big beaks... Their singing encircled the star-apple trunk where Léonce stood, petrified. He wanted to dance, to sing, to whistle a tune he knew. But no sound left his throat. Then he was happy to fill his eyes, his ears and his nostrils with the paradise that his humble garden had become. When his eyes fell on the yam hills, he began to smile to himself. It was miraculous! His smile suddenly broadened, brimmed over and exploded into a hurtling laugh that swung like an acrobat from branch to branch. Unbelievable! Ah! Ah! Greenery aplenty, heralding a miraculous harvest, with flowers twining around poles. Who could have said that those seedlings were so very few months old?

Do dreams often have this appearance of reality? He rubbed his eyes, had a drink of water and looked again. It was at this moment that Octavia appeared. She wore the white dress that covered her bare body the day she died. But, above all, she displayed the youthful face which, eleven years earlier, had made all sorts of Christians wonder, the madames with bitter hearts as well as the simpletons without malice. Her head of white hair was blinding like the midday sun. She smiled at Léonce; it was the smile of a ghost. It silenced the birds in the garden. Terrified, Léonce brandished his hoe. For an instant, he thought of the battle he could wage against Beelzebub and his secret army. But he remembered the deadly weapon which slays demons and he rattled off immediately one 'Our Father' after another. The grandmother's laughter drowned out all trace of his incantation and kept coming closer, closer. When he felt an icy breath drying his cold sweat, he closed his eyes and waited. Let her kill me once and for all! I know that my mamma did not put me on this earth for love, only to suffer and be troubled by gas! My every small pleasure that I enjoy comes at a very high price, which must be paid in cash! No, I was not born for love, only for death...At present, the time has come for Ma Octavia to take me away! Let's be done with it! he thought... But life is a coward. It outruns death. It plays tricks, makes faces, quite a big fuss, just a little while longer...It takes hold of a rope, catches a branch, steals some air, yet a little more life, I beg you. Léonce monkeyed about, swaggered, strutted before the ghost, tried every trick so that death could not get hold of him.

'Ma Octavia! So it is you out there!'

'Ah! Ah! You have recognised me! Don't be afraid, my son...It is just us two, us two! Why do you tremble like that? Have I hurt you, my son? Don't I owe you eternal gratitude?…You were my arms, my legs, when paralysed, crippled by my illness, because of a damned dish of rice and smoked herring, I became once more a baby in my cradle.You see how I am not lying; I did tell you that our paths would cross again. Your heart is good, yes!…I saw you making your little visits to the cemetery. I caressed your face a number of times, I really did, as soon as I found you, both knees on the ground, praying for my soul. You are good people! You took nothing from the side of your mother, Ma Ninette…One All Saints' evening, I placed a little smack on your hand as you were fixing candles on my grave…I laughed loudly. But you heard nothing. I must tell you that, in truth, there are nothing but old dry bones down bottom. I am on another shore that you cannot know…' A young girl's smile played on her lips. Her eyes flickered wildly like moths around a lamp. From her teeth, eaten away by death, flashes of white light darted, brightening her every laugh.

'Listen now!' She blew away a feather floating by, frowned so as to organise the thoughts that drifted through her mind, then she began again, in a hurry, as if the time left was precisely measured. 'Listen, my boy! Your oldest girl will be Célestina. Do not give her any other name! A male youth will be next, but he is not for this world. Tell your dear wife to be patient, not to shed too much water, because she will be sent two, a little before her last offspring. You will have four pickney! Do not ask the Lord for any more! That is

83

your due, no more…And don't go around telling these people that I came to see you…Ah! I was forgetting: I am returning to you the gift that your mamma took away. Take good care of it! Don't abuse it and use it wisely! I have spoken,' she said, before flying off in a cloud of silver and gold.

Léonce gobbled up the words of his dead grand-mother without letting a single one escape. When she disappeared, night fell at that very moment in the garden. The poor fellow gritted his teeth, for he knew that the midday sun was shining bright in the heart of town. He wanted to keep his eyes open but a hand blocked his view. No one knows why, but he fell immediately into a weightless sleep. First, his body was lifted into a sky crossed by shooting comets in which suns gave birth to still-born moons and the stars walked on their outspread points as if on carnival stilts. Then he almost drowned in a sea of black trenches inhabited by drunken moon-fish, brooding seahorses, hermit sea turtles and squid with twenty or thirty tentacles armed with fierce suction pads.

He finally came down in an open field with wild guavas where donkeys, while chewing a blue grass, kicked the air with their hind legs. His eyes followed a hummingbird tasting the hearts of flowers. Then he beat his wings like a yellow butterfly flying off into the distance. That is how he took wing, absent-mindedly. Alas, the wings that he had grown melted in the sun, which had come back out. Seeing the end of the adventure rapidly approaching, he began to pedal in the void. That is what saved him. He fell twenty feet but landed, mercifully, on a donkey. The beast, alas, was wild and threw him off. His head collided with a stone which caused him to enter a short pitch-black sleep, dreamless and painless, a little sleep-baby-sleep. When he awoke, at the foot of the star-apple tree, he pinched the back of his hand, raised an eyelid and stretched his neck to see whether Ma Octavia had really left. Around him, the garden stood motionless, a fork standing here, there a cutlass, lower down a hoe. The garden had no story to tell, revealed no trace of feeling, bore the mark of no memory. Léonce stretched out a leg, rose, stepped over his hat and began to search feverishly the way dogs sniff around. The smell of a witch...a thread, a piece of fabric, caught up in a thorny branch...a hairpin or a safety-pin...a footprint! Yes, a foot and five toes printed in a circle of mud. The sun had returned but it was a wicked sun which cut your skin and burned your eyes. A sun that pierced your back with fine needles and dried your throat. A sun that cracked the bad earth on the hill. The garden was waiting, patiently ...waiting for him to begin tilling. The garden just stood there, motionless, docile, dumb, distant like a woman who allows herself to be taken but feels no love and shows it. Shattered by what he had seen and what was left to be done in order to arrive at a duplication of the extraordinary garden, he returned to sit at the foot of his tree. He had just begun to reflect on the cruelty of dreams that abuse the mind when a star-apple fell on his head. That had the effect on him of the siren that sounded midday right in the heart of town. Then he undid the cord that bound him to the family of tears, complaints and their ilk. He got up and left with a great guffaw. And then he began to run like some mad fellow, scattering confetti on 14 July and unfurling imaginary garlands wherever his laughter drove him. When Myrtha emerged from behind the yam hills, her two hands holding her seven-month belly, he sang out the name of Célestina, his first-born.

X
Breast-fed on Rum

So said, so done: Myrtha gave birth to a girl who was named Célestina in accordance with the very last wishes of Great-grandmother, who had come for precisely this from beyond the grave. Léonce, of course, did not tell anyone about the incredible vision he had had. Not even his Myrtha, who, in the privacy of their bed, questioned him at length about the burst of laughter which made him shoot off his mouth just when she came to meet him. In vain did she slide her probing fingers along his spine, or deep into his navel, or interrogate one by one the thick hairs that made his chest swell, or torment with, 'Ah yes, tell me, my sweetness' his neck and ears, or beg, caress, or pile the kisses on his mouth, clamped shut like a spoilt mollusc. Léonce did not betray Ma Octavia.

A gift, you see, is as delicate as eggnog; eggs sat on for too long, a passing smell of cooking fat, a badly scoured jar, and it's goodbye lock, stock, barrel, eggnog and all! A gift is earth to be gently turned over, without haste, like when you are making pastry at the point of mixing in the egg whites whipped up like snow to the mixture of flour, sugar and yolks. A gift is a little of God's heaven come down to earth. It is a garden of delights with fruit to be guarded – thieves are lurking – its flowers to be adored, its herbs to be weeded…A gift is the union of heaven and earth, it is the arc of a rainbow in the middle of the day.

Léonce was transfigured. You could say a light followed him, showing him the way. His smile was no longer a simple stretching of the mouth, but a bridge of happiness on which his immaculately white teeth danced. His eyes shone with an overwhelming intensity, probed his fellow men and drove the iniquitous far from his sight. His brow was smoother than an exhausted sea after a hurricane. And, even if he continued to walk with a limp…even if he still wore special shoes to walk in the streets of La Pointe, or to go to Christ's meeting-place, no longer did anyone call him Kochi. As for the tiny rasping voice, it simply fell silent, without further ado. On the day the gift was returned to him, a new man was born in the garden on the hill after an overripe star-apple hit him on the skull.

'We will name her Célestina, Octavia, Étiennette.'

'And if it's a boy?'

'I have already told you that you are carrying a girl, Myrtha. Don't ask any more questions!'

'How do you know? Tell me, sweetie!'

'I dreamed it, OK! It was a dream…'

'All the same, look for a boy's name. If you are wrong, he will become a homosexual! It will be all your fault!' cried Myrtha, the very day she gave birth.

When afternoon came, he slipped into a rocking-chair on the veranda, a glass of rum in his hand, savouring the pleasure of a future and certain paternity. The screams of a lost animal that Myrtha uttered did not disturb him. He had the gift. He knew. He could already see his little Célestina, in her mother's lap, greedily sucking on her ample titties, belching the way full bellies do, opening eyes, mouth, ears to take in all the world's knowledge which awaited only her arrival. He was happy. So he poured himself some shots which he drank mechanically, one after the other, and the rum deposited him in Célestina's third year. They were walking on the same hill, hand in hand, just like two loving souls. When the child wanted to see what was happening down below, she leaped on to his back and, with the tip of his finger, he pointed out to her the colourful market with its stalls piled high with fruit and vegetables of all kinds, its flower sellers in their postures as virgins or beggar women. Then, he opened his hand, like a magician in the circus, and the town appeared, behind a big cloud. The cabins gave rise to a century-old pity, a sea of whys, a Soufrière of doubts. Misery groaned there, in the rotting floorboards and the pockmarked zinc roofs, in the mending and the blending, the dishes put out to dry on benches and the clothes put out to bleach on rocks or on the grass. He closed his hand and the town disappeared in a wave of the sea of Haute-Terre, which gnawed, like an obstinate dog, at the same piece of beach for some time, a hundred years, a thousand years maybe.

In the depths of the house, behind the barred door, groans came, went, collided with each other without ill will. Then there was calm. Léonce perked up his ears and breathed a little. No, he ought not to be worried. Myrtha was not alone in this female ordeal. Close to her stood a midwife known throughout Basse-Terre for whom he had sent his cousin Edvard in a vehicle. Ma Ninette was there too, in all her goodness, always willing to assist, to do her bit, to give a little extra of her time, thought Léonce, throbbing with filial gratitude. A short silence lasted a moment, filled with thoughts that drifted with a draught bringing in the smell of the sea. Suddenly, a wild shriek flew out of the cabin and grabbed him by the throat. He quickly poured a large shot of rum, which he drank off with a grimace, so crude was the alcohol. Between the screams of the fortunate woman who bore his offspring, you could hear the scraping of pans and the muffled voices of the older women. He listened closely once again before swallowing another mouthful of rum. What! Someone was opening the door! A scream...No! It must be a mouse caught in the rat-trap. Léonce was living his Golgotha. He felt like crap, little-little, like stale food. His flesh became soft. His insides swarmed with wild activity. A fever transported him to a land of ice. An ocean swept him away like a jellyfish's umbrella. He died and was born again the third day after Christmas, mad, like a pig bled dry, browned and eaten to celebrate Jesus Christ. He was returning to avenge all his fellow pigs sacrificed to the Lamb of God, ever since folks sucked on black pudding, like a woman's breast, voraciously. Only the rum brought him some relief, building in him, little by little, a feeling of self-importance. When Célestina's screams finally broke the darkness of the evening, the town clock chimed six o'clock. The wailing of the new-born was mixed with the pealing of the bells. Léonce heard neither cries nor chimes, only a big drum pounding, banging, throbbing in his chest.

Ninette found the rocking-chair empty. Where could Léonce be hiding? She stumbled against a dark mass balled up on the floor. Was it that stray dog again, which turned up from God knows where and saw

Myrtha as its salvation because she threw it a few bones? The creature uttered a sigh, stretched slowly. An empty bottle rolled beside it, bounced against the railing and rolled unsteadily until it crashed into a rock in the yard. The sky suddenly began to play tricks, as an army of clouds swept in looking like wild Africans spitting fireworks and muffled thunder. The rain came down heavily and Ninette recognised her Léonce in a flash of lightning. A dog! She had lowered her son to the level of a runaway dog! Bad omen... The rain blew on to the veranda. Ninette shook the fellow, blind drunk with rum, and carefully administered two-three good slaps. Léonce opened one eye and valiantly tried to get into an upright position. A waste of time. He could only drag himself on four feet across to the rocking-chair, so distant, like a boat calmly proceeding on its course before the yellowing gaze of some shipwrecked soul.

'The Lord has given you a daughter, Léonce!'

'I know, I know...' he grumbled. 'Ma Octavia already told me all that.'

'A pretty little girl, pretty pretty, yes! Are you hearing?' Ninette was whispering as if there was a dead body in the house. 'You will go and splash some water on your face, to revive yourself, eh! And you will go to see her... What is the matter with you? You are not going to hit the bottle, eh! You are not going to succumb to the black man's vice!'

Ma Ninette kept on talking... and Léonce, capsized in the armchair, which was drunkenly rocking, felt he was in the open sea, in the middle of the raging waters of the passage of Les Saintes. When did he end up in this canoe? Seasick, that's what he was! He must take control of this canoe as quickly as possible in order to get back to the safety of dry land, where he could walk, he thought. Then he thought of his lunch, which he brought up at that very time. And Ninette was hit in the face by an eruption of chewed-up figs and minced meat from his unruly bowels. His stomach empty, Léonce felt light, his mind clear. He left the boat of drunkenness and discovered, in a single image, his mother's face. He took a few steps on the veranda and reached the yard, across which spread great pools of water like mirrors. A lingering shower finally dried up the heavens. Léonce washed his face and rinsed out his mouth with the drips from the zinc roof. All the while, Ninette was splashing herself with water from a barrel, cursing the viciousness of the local whites who extracted this rum poison from the innocent sugar cane. More than anything in the world, more than Sosthène's infidelities, she loathed the fellows who sucked on the breast of rum. But the sky was now dry. Five or six stars, lights from another world, twinkled like will-o'-the-wisps at the edge of the cemetery. Léonce sat down, crying, on a wet stone.

He engaged in an excited prattling with himself:

'So, Léonce! That is how you behave...a gift has been bestowed on you and you allow the Devil to possess your spirit! Your body is a temple and you defile it by getting drunk like some indecent person!

'I swear! I did not even see when I took down the bottle from the sideboard.'

'Liar! I read your mind! You went on like this: "I am all-powerful, I have the gift! I know that my Myrtha will not die giving birth, that I will have a girl who will be named Célestina, Octavia, Étiennette. I know my past and my future will be revealed to me through the mouth of my good granny Octavia."'

'Forgive me, my Lord! I am a poor sinner. Pardon, O Eternal Father who reigns in eternity for century after century...'

Ma Octavia appeared suddenly, before him, with the glow of the Holy Virgin. Léonce was startled.

'Is that all you can say: "I'm sorry, Lord!" and off you go to kiss wife and child, with simply this little "excuse me" to salve your conscience!'

'Am I completely lost, Mamma?'

Léonce panicked; Octavia's face was not laughing.

'Promise me one thing!'

'OK! OK! I give you my word... before God, before man... before yesterday's, today's and tomorrow's heaven... before you, my guardian, my shield, my good Ma Octavia. Ugh...! I swear on my honour that never-more shall the diabolical juice of the cane make its way down my throat and end up deep in my stomach ... May I leave this world of the living the very instant my oath gets soaked in the water of falsehood...'

'You have given your word, Léonce! That's good, you may go... but you must keep your promise! If not...! Dry your eyes now and go!'

His peace of mind restored, Léonce entered the room where Myrtha was lying. When he saw the child, a surge of emotion took hold of his body. He fell on his knees.

XI
Pathos, Pallet, Pickney

And Sosthène, could you tell me, what is happening with him while his son is communicating with spirits all the time and discovering the joys of paternity? Papa Sosthène was beginning to realise that he had not swallowed the potion of eternal youth. So this is old age! One day when he was shaving himself mechanically, he began, as a joke, to count his wrinkles, he ventured to calculate his white hairs — more than the day before and much less than tomorrow's. Then he measured the width of his bald spot, examined his thickening skin. And then he noticed that his back no longer straightened to his satisfaction and that his legs, formerly reliable when walking, no longer took him where he wanted to go. Alas! he thought, time is going by and even fiery roosters can become senile, good for stewing and not for screwing! Just yesterday, he felt he still wore his rooster's feathers, still was king of his hen house, courted by some tempting chicks. Not so long ago, he often went wandering off to the edge of the plantations to have a look, in the cane fields, at the haunches of the women tying the bundles. At will, he took them. A glance, sweet talk tickled their pumpums, one hand caressed their titties, the other lifted their skirt and it was all over. It's the honest truth, Sosthène did not need a whole heap of appetisers to get to the main meal. The women were laid, gave their bodies to this fellow of few words, wiggled their pelvises and sighed aaah!!! Alas, the adulterous deed signed and sealed, Sosthène would jump up, pick two-three leaves from a branch to wipe off his notorious prick, pull up his drawers along with his pants and angrily tie the cord that served as a belt. He no longer knew the one he had just laid. So he directed neither word, nor look, nor excuse, nor promise at the poor woman drunk with pleasure who did not yet know that the rascal had stuck in her the egg of ill-luck, cubits of misfortune and three rivers of tears. He ran off, shirt flying in the wind. Never looking back. More often than not pursued by all manner of curses which tore at his back, pounded away at him and smashed the back of his neck. Then a headache took hold of him. He reached the end of his journey staggering. Once in the house, he fell on his knees, pulled down the Bible from the shelf and launched into a prayer of repentance.

So, imagine that one day he was in such a situation: at the edge of a plantation, the consenting female in the cane piece... And then! Nothing... His legendary maleness, so dishonest, remained limp... Absolutely limp. The young woman's laughter cackled harshly, like blows from a cudgel, before the appendage that felt not the slightest emotion. He stood there, helpless, before the brown, scented patch of hair under which was hidden, beyond any doubt, a wide bottomless well. And this time, this last time, when he ran off, it was not curses that scratched at his back but the wild laughter of a young black female without panties, the laughter of an army of Prussians before his Waterloo. The spell was broken.

It was from this day forward that Sosthène fell into a melancholy state. Believe it, his undoing brought relief to Ninette. Imagine! She was already forty-eight and he was in his sixties. Now a grandmother, the woman had taken in his daily seed, without flinching, for twenty-five years... Twenty-five years of submission in the marriage bed! Twice times ten plus five years of faking willingness and heat (when in reality she was like marble), praying to the Virgin Mary that her forced eagerness would bring her philandering husband back to the straight and narrow path of fidelity. A quarter of a century – can you imagine! – of spreading, each evening, her legs in the darkness in order to receive the tainted nectar from this indefatigable scamp... Yes, twenty-five years that the mattress had been asking for mercy.

The first time Sosthène turned his back to her in bed, instead of hugging her as he usually did, Ninette really thought that one of her dreams had become reality. The following morning she woke with a long-forgotten sense of renewal. During the day, she took to humming and whistling, as if nothing was amiss. She walked to and fro in front of her old Sosthène, without seeing him, without even looking at him, without ever asking him the time of day. He remained glued to the house. When evening came, she went to bed before him and, in the dark, kept her eyes open. That evening, once again, he dumped his beaten carcass on the old bed and presented the scales on his back for her to admire. The following morning, Ninette announced Sosthène's humiliation. She did not jump up and down, oh no. She had known for a long time that if there was a going, there would also be a coming around. Sosthène was in his turn-around. Well, you know how they are, these people who speak with their eyes, gestures and sighs. One fine morning, the wife rolled and tied up the old mattress, its covering darkened by a whole heap of nauseating secretions. She shouted to two little boys from next door who, one in front and the other behind, carried it to Mister Berlow, English and a mattress–maker by trade. Those who remember this day will tell you that the spectacle was worth it. You had to see Ninette under her umbrella, proud like a police officer on parade, leading the procession. The two youths who were bearing the mattress behaved like employees of a funeral parlour. The mattress on their heads, they walked ceremoniously, their faces solemn and their gait deliberate. Three days later, Ninette picked up a new mattress. She had chosen a covering of pink satin with a flowery pattern and had demanded that the soiled cotton be combed out not once but twice.

When the mattress appeared, Ninette began a new life. And Sosthène sank deeper into his melancholy. He no longer climbed on to the marriage bed, preferring the hard floor, on to which he threw each evening rags and crocus bags. Ma Ninette didn't give a damn, like a queen with her lowest servant. What else do you expect! She had not made a case in her own defence when the sea breezes swelled the sails of her unfaithful husband, pushing him always further from her shore.

She was not now going to take up Jesus Christ's cross and feel pity because Sosthène's life force did not shine with all its fire...

So, she spread out on the bed, opened arms and legs

wide and slept through the night. In the morning she rose fresh like a maiden, gave two-three kicks to the ribs of the fellow having problems and set about doing her work, her brow unruffled, her heart at ease.

The children were grown. They had all gone their separate ways, taken up their responsibilities. The boys had chosen their wives and Lucina was making her way at La Pointe. Only Sosthène remained. Alas, the fellow had fallen into a laziness like you wouldn't believe. The only thing he moved was wind. With great effort, he deposited his backside on a bench and, for the entire day, leafed through the Bible with its thousands of parables. His face had the very look of an abandoned garden, attacked by a savage onslaught of bitter weeds. Monstrous and solid, just like the large rocks of La Soufrière, his hair piled up around the crater of his bald patch. In no time, his flesh was taken over by a listless old body, tired of living, sickly and trembling. Death's outspread wings already shadowed his steps and sometimes beat against him. He sank a little deeper into melancholy when he thought of the parcels piled up for him outside the door of purgatory. If the Lord opened them at this very moment, he would not find anything clean, he thought. Nothing but sin... mud from a sugar-cane field, scratches from chabine women, visions of pum-pums, limp cocks, longings for thighs, thrusts, tearing, scandals and prayers, 'Our Father's, drawers turned inside out, phials, the scent of ilang-ilang, a Mona, some Lucys, Merediths, Hortenses and Hortensias... red poppies of lies, tears of laid females and wailing children...Some 'Ave Maria's, some blessings, five-finger-Éléonore standing in a field, her heart like a crossbow, the marble cracked and the candle soaked...Tell me, good Lord, tell me, what you are doing to me!...

Ninette did some dishes, swept a little, without even seeing Sosthène's shadow. And then she left the house, humming merrily on the way to Léonce's hillside, where Célestina grew without a hitch, surrounded by her parents' love. With the birth of that child, Ninette had found a goal in life. Hector had given her, with the aid of his Indian wife, four little Indian pickney but Célestina alone made her eyes light up. Hector's pickney left her cold, seemed to be refugees from misery, products of animal unions. Ever since Hector set up house with her, the girl never stopped procreating. Year after year, Ninette saw her belly swell and throw out, stretch and produce. She harboured sorrow in the whites of her eyes, as if to say that the earth was a heavy load and that she would do no better than the good Lord's son. They called her Agatha. She looked after her pickney in a don't-care way, gave them food like a mother pig, dressed them only on the Lord's day and let them play naked, all day long, in the yard. When Ninette, who had sacrificed to raise hers in spite of misery and the blows dealt by fate, tried to instil basic maternal feelings in her, Agatha shrugged a shoulder and replied:

'Is little pickney! Them don't need anything but food, doodoo, weewee, sleepy! These children are OK,

Ma Nine. Don't worry yourself about them!'

Ninette was no wiser when it came to Hector's attitude. He looked at his offspring without really seeing them. He smoked his pipe and reflected on this, then meditated on that, reasoned about the essence of being, sheep's brains, the white man's mysteries and the black man's spirits. 'He is philosophising, philosophising!' Ninette complained. 'But he does not see that time has come to add another two rooms to his cabin!'

For almost a year Célestina was the light of Ninette's life. Each morning, since Sosthène's undoing, and no matter what the weather, she left her house and set off to join the source of her light like the wise men following the star of Bethlehem. She climbed the hill effortlessly and went away at nightfall. It was a habit she had acquired, a kind of existence she had adopted. At the outset, Myrtha felt relieved. And then she realised that Ninette had become the mistress of her house. Léonce's mother put her mouth in everything, gave orders, advice, criticism and condemnation. What Myrtha did was never to her liking, deserved to be improved, fell short of perfection. She then added her ifs, buts and maybes. She stole each burp, each kiss and the dressing-up of Célestina, whom she snatched from her mother's arms, because she knew how to do everything better. And Léonce approved of everything, said amen to every word that issued from Ninette's mouth. Myrtha began to grumble to herself and swell up like a frog. Léonce did not see a thing. So she clamped her mouth tight, like a chicken's bottom, since no one listened to her any more. While Léonce believed that happiness had overwhelmed her, deep wrinkles furrowed her brow and she covered her eyes with a spider's web. Léonce got his first warning; Ma Octavia came down with the express purpose of opening his eyes:

'What is the use of your having a gift, Léonce? Can't you see that Myrtha is shrivelling up because of Ninette! Really, how blind can you get! Even if it is your mother... Today, I am forced to tell you a few things about her. When you were a poor little innocent she wanted to take away the gift the Lord had bestowed on you... She ground up the caul as much as she could... So hear me now, if you do not stop her little game this very moment, you will soon find yourself with your head in your hands, weeping in ruin and loneliness. Let her go take care of her skirt-chaser of a husband instead of messing up your future. Myrtha is already carrying the boy who is not for this world. Something bad is eating her insides. She will lose this child, as I told you. Take heart! Do what you have to, the time is now...' And then Octavia disappeared in a sigh, eyes lowered. That night, seated on his bed, Léonce spent much time wondering whether he had dreamed these words.

XII
Miraculous Hands

The coffin of white wood struck the earth in the cemetery with the snapping sound of a nut being cracked. Once again, Myrtha dried her tears. She never got to know him, this poor infant who tore her flesh and, for only two months, sucked the little milk she had. Two little months of life and this big death…On that day, she had occasion to feel the helplessness that comes from three centuries of grief. That is exactly what she felt, standing before the grave. Three centuries of grief, three generations of sorrow: birth, bonding and burial. Three centuries of grief…this thought aggravated the misfortune and waved incessantly, before her eyes, the dead face of her son. Since morning she had banded her breasts. The milk still dripped through, staining her black dress. He is hungry in his coffin, she thought. The milk sprang throughout the day like grass that you just could not destroy. The milk did not want to dry up. And her heart was immersed in a sorrow that knew no bounds. She wept at the sight of a pot, a living bird, a star at night. One day, she no longer wished to get up out of bed and began to waste away quietly.

Léonce futilely took her hand, put food in her mouth and tried to give back to her exhausted body the sweet taste of the small pleasures of this world. Myrtha did not emerge from this nothingness.

'The next time, you will have a pair of children…' he whispered to her, sure of what he said. Goat mouth, Ma Octavia had predicted it and everything that came out of her mouth was pure truth, Holy Scriptures. Why had he not listened more closely? A feather from the roof would occasionally settle on the bed, above Myrtha's head. Was this Octavia indicating her presence?

'Sweetie, come back, come back! Your body has not stopped producing. Soon, believe me, for nine moons two twin hearts will beat in your breast!' Léonce cried, glancing from time to time through the open window at the moon, silent just like Myrtha. But above all, he talked to bring her back to him, hoping that these words placed end to end, with infinite patience, would form the steps of a solid staircase that, one step at a time, Myrtha would climb in order to leave the dark where the death of her second child had cast her.

Alas, he continued to give his blessing to his mother, who played the roles of king and queen in Myrtha's house. Célestina was exposed to her tender words and her unwholesome thoughts. And in her state of limbo, Ma Octavia grew mad at seeing the great misfortune that befell the hill like the rain of Apocalypse. Somewhere, far away, she paced up and down cursing and blaspheming. On several occasions, Léonce tried to convince his mother to take better care of Papa Sosthène. But he could not find the words to say it. He asked himself: had Ma Via really come? He must have been dreaming...his mind had perhaps created this threat that hung over his head... 'Ruin and solitude!' the grandmother had said.

'Is Ma Ninette the cause of this great anguish?' he asked himself one evening.

These two-three words had an instant effect. Some kind of fit took hold of Myrtha. Her body suddenly grew stiffer than a plank from the Stinking Toe tree and levitated up, up above the bed, remained suspended for a moment and then came back down.

Her eyes became white and terrifying. Léonce threw himself over to the other side of the cabin, instinctively – or because of a survival instinct – he made the sign of the cross, did a laying-on of hands, called to his side Jesus Christ, Our Lady of Providence, Saint Anne and the Holy Spirit, Ecclesiastes, Ezekiel, God the Father. Then he cleared the air with a dry palm from last Easter and sprinkled the corners with the remaining drops of ammonia. He came and went, impotent, crazed, undone. He leaped up each time Myrtha levitated and got on his knees when she came back down again. His vision was clouded by tears. His mouth choked with prayers. And Myrtha rose, stiff, and then came back down again. It was already three months that she no longer left her bed and spat back out the soup that Ninette prepared. Words seemed to die in her throat. Is it not time to put my gift into action? thought Léonce.

'Ma Octavia, Ma Vie!' he murmured. His voice dripped with tears. 'Ma Vivie, come and help me! Why have you forsaken me?' Beads of oily sweat formed at his temple. 'I know that you are hearing me. I know you are very angry…'

'Did I not tell you to get rid of your mother! So what, I am talking to the wind!'

The grandmother appeared at the bed-head.

'Save her for my sake, Ma Vie…have pity!' groaned Léonce, his two knees on the ground.

Ma Octavia looked at the young woman, took hold of the bedposts and slowly – with a breath blown from

108

the world beyond – pushed the evil out of Myrtha's body. She rose one last time, straining, seemed to hesitate, caught between two currents, and then fell back, limp, on the soft bed.

'Do what you must, Léonce! You have waited too long!!!' With these words, Octavia disappeared in a rustling of razor grass. A cock crowed three times.

When later on in the morning, Ma Ninette climbed the hill and found the doors of the cabin shut, she assumed, without thinking, that a premature widowhood had flattened Léonce. In truth, when she thought of it... the previous evening, Myrtha did seem weaker. As if life had no more meaning and she was more tired than a hundred-year-old grandmother surrounded by an army of children, grandchildren and great-grandchildren. Immediately, Ninette's mind began to race. Poor Léonce, she thought, so young and to lose like this the sunshine of his days. What do you expect? The plans of the Almighty are mysterious, everyone knows that. She would take care of the orphan girl, her dear CéCé. But in truth, where was Célestina? And Léonce!... She put her ear to the door that opened on to the veranda. Nothing. She circled the house. No sound, no noise. She climbed on an empty saltfish box. She knocked on the closed blinds and listened closely. Nothing! My God, should she race to the hospital, the church or even the cemetery? It was then she heard the sound of laughter coming from the garden. She lifted her skirts and headed off in the direction of the voices. They were all there, a beautiful family: Myrtha, her health miraculously restored, her complexion like new, her eyes clear, her cheeks round; Célestina, frolicking like a goat kid among the tree trunks; and, in this sweet picture, her Léonce, smiling like a big imbecile, lunching on yam and pumpkin pickles. Léonce was expecting his mother. He had understood everything, even if quite late. He had prepared some wise words in order to, at the same time, satisfy Ma Octavia's orders and avoid hurting Ninette's excessive touchiness. He started the very moment she appeared.

'Ohoh! It's you, Mamma! We were waiting for you to tell you how grateful we are. From now on, you will no longer have to worry about us and force yourself to climb, each day made by God, this hill too steep for your bones. You will no longer have to concern yourself with Myrtha. Look! Have a look at what your good care has done! Look at how solid she is today! You can work miracles, Ma Ninette! Yes, it's really true...Perhaps you can save my papa!' suggested Léonce, tearing into a pickle. 'God speaks through you, Mamma! You are a miracle worker...I think your hands are miraculous.'

Myrtha lifted her eyes to heaven and sent a prayer to the angels passing by. Fear gripped her heart. She did not know the woman deeply, if not she would have known that the danger was taken care of. The girl did not know that Ninette had a little of the poli-trickster in her. She did not promise Panamas, job sites, an independence that had been seized, a future of respect, work at the town hall or a space in the poor-house. But like them she did not get emotional about anything and cultivated the gift of the gab. She had their skill, their versatility, a hint of contempt, an innate condescension, an obsession with grand sentences, an unseemly elitism and a know-it-all look that said 'I am the Messiah come to save you.' So, at the moment when Léonce swallowed his last pickle, Ninette draped herself in the skin of Saint Ma Ninette, patron of the very ill, saviour of the depressed, God's hand on those whose flesh was bruised.

Perhaps you believe that all this is a tall tale and this quickly sketched scene bears no relation to the honest truth. That is how it was told to me. Rest assured that not a comma, not a word, not even a pickle was removed or added. And when she hugged to her bosom her first miracle, Ninette was completely transformed. Her eyes sparkled, sometimes glittering with flashes of goodness. And her face shone with a pure selflessness that had been copied from the Blessed Virgin. When she went back down the hill that morning, wings in the air, her feet no longer touched the ground, so much had her new body, as patron saint of the sick with no hope of tomorrow, given a lightness to her mortal flesh.

On her way back, Léonce's voice continued to echo in her ears: 'God is speaking in you! You are perform-ing wonders, Mamma! Your hands are miraculous!' Her calling became firmly anchored. Back home, a desire for a massive cleaning-up took hold of her, like divine inspiration. She found Sosthène sitting on a bench, mumbling verses.

'Get up and walk!' she ordered.

For months now, the man had all the mannerisms of a fellow who was cast out of the human race. Immediately, he got up, as if he had been poked in the back with a stick. He took three steps towards Ninette, who was enjoying her triumph as master before her well-trained dog.

'You smell like old smoked meat!' she said spitefully, before resuming a look of humility. 'What am I going to do with you? Lord Almighty, give me strength! I'm going to wash you, cut your hair and trim that beard a bit. Put the bench under the almond tree!' Sosthène obeyed. She made him undress behind the cabin and set about scrubbing him. She tore off, as it were, a long-standing layer of filth, thick like pork rind. When she undertook to wash his noble body parts, Sosthène was shaken by a great shudder. Up to that point, he had maintained a sheep-like docility. It was as if, all of a sudden, life returned to him. Some sort of throbbing on the surface of his skin. The raising of an eyebrow. A new rush of air into the lungs. A jolt to the heart. A flame reviving his prick. Having gone off to fetch water, Ninette found on her return a Sosthène as rejuvenated as if he were a twenty-year-old. She was dumbfounded. Léonce's words sounded even more loudly in her ears... 'God is talking through you! You can perform wonders! Your hands are miraculous!' At present, this great truth was displayed for all eyes to see.

From that day, Ninette no longer walked in the streets of Haute-Terre unless dressed in a white cloth and wearing on her head a great square of cotton fabric cut from a flour bag. That is how everyone knew that she had taken vows and devoted herself to God in her virgin purity. She made Sosthène promise not to mount her any more. Which he did without asking why. Soon, the assuring news that her hands could heal was borne on the wind. Cripples of all races began to arrive from a thousand places in Guadeloupe. They came from far to receive some relief, crowded on to the benches, chatting all the while in hushed voices about the terrible ills that afflicted them, more often than not the doing of sorcerers and the work of envious people.

The day Léonce announced to her that Myrtha had just brought into the world a pair of infants called Paul and Céluta, Ninette had to scrimp time between two sessions to give them her blessing.

XIII
The Break of 1937

Léonce put such an effort into his garden that it had almost become a replica of the extraordinary garden glimpsed the day of Grandma Octavia's first appearance. Naturally, the trees did not yet touch the sky, the fruits were not being produced by the ton or by the thousand. But the bunches exploded in the outstretched fingers of the branches. Under the earth, the tubers were growing thick. And the birds sang, flew about, giving man courage for the work to be done.

Célestina was almost four. The twins had just turned two. And Gerty the last girl was greedily sucking her mother's milk. In her ignorance, Myrtha thought of still giving another two-three children to her family. Léonce did not argue with her. He knew that Gerty had closed the door behind her. One after the other Léonce had seen his grandmother's prophecies come true. Octavia had declared: 'There will be four of them, do not demand any more of the Almighty!' So, what was the point of pleading with the heavens, the earth and his Myrtha's insides. He ought to be happy with his one and only son, Paul, a temperamental child inhabited by a tormented spirit.

In this year 1937, Léonce celebrated his twenty-fourth birthday. His body had grown even stronger. His features became more pronounced from day to day. He entered, as it were, a kind of maturity. What about his club-foot? you say to me. Who cared about that now! Right in the heart of town and in the surrounding hills, it was fully understood that the fellow enjoyed the kind of protection that made him reap the fruits of an everlasting good fortune...Bags of money under the mattress! Gold in the cupboards locked away up there in those hills! And even if he continued to get up at dawn to plant and dig (although he could have, without any trouble, paid someone to work the garden!), even if he himself always sold his fruits and vegetables at the main market at Pointe-à-Pitre (instead of making an arrangement with a retailer), it was known that he did it more out of pleasure and habit than necessity. His business was just fine and dandy. As soon as he appeared in town, his customers immediately stopped their dealings and abandoned the stalls of the other vendors. In no time, his purse jingled with a thousand coins. The more he sold, the more his baskets were replenished. You could say his goods were never ending. That year he added three rooms to his cabin on the hill. And then he bought some fertile land from an old spinster schoolteacher who wanted to bury her mother without touching her savings sleeping in a bank at La Pointe. The woman had told him that if a black man, in this instance Félix Éboué, had been named governor of the colonies, you could no longer swear for anything. She therefore had to take measures beforehand, just in case...

The house on the hill was the spitting image of Myrtha, always spruced up, always happy. At this time, who could have reminded her of the wanderings of her youth, the misery of her parents and the cramped hovels eaten out by termites. When Léonce got her first sewing machine for her, she immediately learned to sew and produced, out of the mystery of her fantasies as a young girl, tablecloths, napkins, curtains, embroidered sheets, pillowcases with wide lace borders, bedspreads with large flowers and small leaves. Quite naturally she began to make clothes. First of all for the children and then for Léonce, finally for herself. Each Sunday the family was dressed in new clothes. Myrtha glowed, with the pickney at her feet and Léonce on her arm. Too bad if her beauty blinded the bad-minded scamps who looked at her and winked, she knew where her heart lay and who poured honey on the days of her life. No, Léonce did not look bad next to her. Four years of marriage, already. Sometimes, she recalled the stony path where, a bucket on her head, she passed early in the morning. How many times had he spied on her from down in the ditch? He never spoke to her about this time when love and death tugged at the same body. And she thought that if Léonce was not the man destined for her, he looked just like him. Because of him, she had become wife, mother and property owner... Everything was fine, except... Damn!... she often had the feeling that someone was watching her every move, held her on a leash and directed her to cook such and such a dish on certain days, to cut a dress just so, to punish the children in this way or that. Sometimes, she turned around sharply. One afternoon she was just in time to see a shadow flying away. Was it a spirit, her guardian angel or else the shadow of a bird? There was also that older woman who roamed the hillside. The dry season always brought her back with the heat. She hid her face and fled like a mongoose as soon as Myrtha called out to her. Apart from these mysteries, life flowed sweetly with Ninette away, doing excellently in her new calling...A slight pat, a caress, what should I say, the merest touch and, in great haste, evil rushed out of bodies wild with gratitude. In no time, the chief obeahmen of the town were cleaned out, chased away by the new craze that had taken hold of the people of the town, from all around and even from La Pointe. Would you believe, they came by the truckload in order to receive: cures, comfort, oils and blessings from the good Mamma Ninette. Once upon a time they had a reputation, now her rivals' dispensaries faced a crisis, then went under. Naturally, these envious fixers-of-business tried to band together to destroy the holy woman. An old-timer told the story of the war between good and evil which was declared during this hurricane season. Good Mother Ninette fought them off one after the other. She cleaved in twain dragons whatever their size and crushed underfoot the serpents imported from Martinique. She mocked the white crabs which would turn up at sunset and the puffed-up toads with their mouths padlocked that she found at any time of day in the vicinity of her cabin. The old fellow also remembered a terrible night...a ball of fire had suddenly entered the firmament of the healer and she battled until dawn, armed only with a bronze crucifix. Another time, she found a tiny coffin filled with rotting flesh deposited on her drawing-room couch. All she had to do was to lay on her miraculous hands for a bright light to flash suddenly and take away in its flames the accursed article. It was later revealed that the Holy Virgin herself came down in Ninette's yard, in order to restore peace. It was only from this divine intervention onwards that Haute-Terre regained the peace of times past.

Pa Sosthène, let us get back to him, began to work for the priest. His prick put to sleep in his drawers washed with holy water (an absolutely obligatory ritual), he did everything from A to Z at the presbytery. He was gardener, mason when necessary, occasional cabinetmaker, carpenter, amateur cook. And on Sundays, dressed in white from head to toe, he picked up the collection from the faithful. Fate would have it that during the offering, the women he had impregnated in the past glared at him, pinched his hand and pushed away his basket so roughly that the coins would jingle in it. Sometimes his eyes made one with the eyes of a virgin with his kind of behind, but he no longer felt anything or perhaps...the sensation of a memory impossible for him to bring to light...the hint of something nice that he once knew and which was lost, in sin, like Adam his eternal life.

And during this time, Ma Octavia, looking on from the nether regions, bad-mouthed and cursed the damn fools of Haute-Terre who elevated her daughter Étiennette – called Good Mother Ninette – to the order of those useless female healers of the dry coconut.

A Time for Coming Around

I
Hurricane, Tricentenary and War

So, the winds of war, worse than the hurricane of 1928,
turned Europe upside down... In 1928, the Devil
spoke in the heavens, he spat, cursed and struck. He
swallowed a bitter wind and, out of wickedness, blew
his poisonous breath in the face of the people who
knuckled under or simply stood gaping in the middle

of the arc of Caribbean islands. Does a tree without roots have enough weight to resist a fierce blow from the wind? Black people then lived at the edge of 'If it's God's will!', of 'So be it!' They headed towards a tomorrow of hope which was caught in the sticky glue of destiny. They travelled about according to the whims of contract work, the seasons, on the lands of local whites. The hurricane piled them up at the gates of La Pointe, quite close to the Darboussier factory and the wharf which awaited their manpower. After the hurricane, few houses remained intact. The un-fortunate ones carried off those that the wind rejected. In 1928, the hurricane rerouted rivers, which proceeded to drown human beings and animals alike. Our sea, driven wild in turn, crashed its waves into the earth. Flashes of lightning rent its veil and the sky opened, black. 'We are coming to the dawn of the last days!' announced the old people, looking on the ravaged colony the day after this bacchanal. Through God's mercy, Sosthène's cabin had been miraculously spared. Only five sheets of zinc had taken flight, under the eyes of Ninette, curled up under a high bed. The poor woman took care of her pickney on her own while everything was being turned inside out. Sosthène had not made an appearance for three days and she wondered whether he was not dead in some hole. While the hurricane opened its eye over Haute-Terre, she forced the children to pray for the repose of the soul of their poor papa. Alas! He emerged from the dark, the evening of the following day, dry as can be. In these wretched times when black folks walked on all fours in the ditch of despair, Léonce turned sixteen. Myrtha had not yet crossed his path. And those two did not yet know that it was written that they would be married in 1933, just two years before the celebration of the Tricentenary of the French takeover of Guadeloupe and the erection of the Holy Cross on pagan soil. All of 1935 was one long celebration: folkloric ballets, military parades, high mass, lectures and speeches, fanfare and the laying of wreaths, balls, banquets, toasts, peals of bells and singing, scouts and pennants, majorettes and pom-poms.

The Tricentenary high mass was celebrated at Soufrière, on 30 September 1935. The faithful came running from all the parishes. To tell the truth, Mr Tricentenary had become a kind of popular saint. Many a humble soul, even if they did not know his face or his spot in the cemetery, prayed to him with fervour and faith. He was said to be able to heal strange wounds and knew how to bandage the misery of the wretched. Léonce, Myrtha, Pa Sosthène and Good Mother Ninette walked among the pilgrims. They had taken the night route, lighting their way with the flame from a torch. In the morning, a big crowd scaled along with them the sides of the volcano, young and old alike, led by the mountain-climbing club. At nine-thirty exactly, all the bells in the land rang out at one go. And those who, at a disadvantage, never managed to lift their souls up to the heights of Soufrière, prayed in unison for Our Lady of France,

Guadeloupe her daughter and the Christian church. Ma Ninette, all dressed in white (she was about to take her vows), her face lifted to the Almighty, a rosary coming and going between her fingers, joined her voice with those of hundreds of believers, gathered for the pomp and ceremony of the mass on the mountain top. The hymn of divine inspiration, signed A.B. from Abymes and sung to the tune 144 of the E. Dubois edition, rose towards the heavens:

'For three hundred years, Christians and French
On to Soufrière, having gained access,
Let's swear by these names, promise of success,
To remain Christian and French.

Let us pray on these rocks
While all around
The sounds of our bells
Ring in our towns.

Let us pray to the earth
Where over there sleep
Our dead from the war
who tasted defeat.

Let us pray for that priest
Who was Richelieu by name.
He made us here celebrate
France and her Faith...'

Suddenly, in the middle of this eruption of faith, in the middle of these chants that made the volcano tremble...

'For those who suffered
Obscure pioneers
For those who fell
Here before all

Let us salute the star
Queen of the sea
Which guided their sails
This foresaken place to see...'

...In the middle of the Holy Eucharist of the Tricentenary, Léonce saw his grandmother Octavia appear. She stood upright, behind Father Offendo. Her raucous voice rose...

'Let us pray for the breeze
For the good curate
Dear to our Church
Dear to our spiritual state...'

Léonce staggered, but did not collapse. Someone held him up. When he turned around his gaze met, haloed in a corner of the sky, Octavia's young, fresh face.

'You have hardly come to visit my tomb these last days,' she grumbled. 'Do you wish to turn your back on destiny? Last All Saints' day, you placed a candle hurry-hurry between two conch shells and you dashed off like that, without even reciting a little prayer for the salvation of my soul!'

'But rain was falling, Gramma!'

She laughed. 'You think you smart, eh! Go ahead, sing!'

'Let us pray for the glory
Of those humble souls
Who made history
And who we don't know.

For those soldiers
Those sailors with skill
Those missionaries
Doing God's will…'

'But, but… what are you doing here, Ma Octavia?'
stammered Léonce.

'I am watching over you, my child!

Let heaven's sweet Queen
Christian and French
For us all one day intervene
With the Prince of Peace…'

'Why are you here, Gramma?'

Octavia hesitated a moment. 'I came down to this
spot to give you some advice. Listen!' She lowered her
voice. 'A time of Apocalypse is coming. In a year, or
two, or four maybe, you will better understand what I
am saying. Buy in bulk, and without delay, barrels of
dried cod and pork. Buy up large amounts of sugar
and salt. Fill bags with good roasted coffee. And plant
as of now food for your children. Do not leave even
an inch of ground untouched! Plant herbs that cure
old sores; medicine will become scarce. And tell your
spouse to make jam from fruits and vegetables of all
kinds. Take her to La Pointe. Give her the means to

buy cloth by the metre and by the length, leather for shoes...' She sighed. 'Léonce, I solemnly say to you today – and may Soufrière spit out ashes on the hour if I am lying! – while hearts are happy around here, on the other side of the sea, a man of hatred is rising. His emblem is a hooked cross. He will crush, dominate, annihilate. And his rage will be like that of the slavers of times past...Do not fear for your brothers. Black folks, this time, will know neither exile, nor chains...The offspring of those who killed Jesus Christ will pay a heavy price.'

The mass was coming to an end. Only Léonce could see Octavia. And he remained for a long time, kneeling on the ground, amidst the curious, mumbling between his teeth words with neither beginning nor end in which was repeated like the throbbing sound of a boula drum these terrible words: 'War! War! War!'

1939. Europe was heading for war and even in the midst of the colonies could be heard the explosions of the wretched German bombs. A new idol imposed its order and sacrificial rites. Its cross was the swastika, its doctrine was like iron and before its totem crowds bowed down. Europe was breaking wind and its gases, pushed by the trade winds, fouled up the air in our lands. Europe, cleaved in twain by the angel from hell, fought on its knees and the people from the sugar islands bled like stuck pigs at Christmas. In France, Marshal Pétain signed the Armistice and divided the country in two. In Guadeloupe, the governor, Constant Sorin, sucked the last drop of blood from black people. 'Work!' he said. 'Work! Take the trouble! Sow, you shall reap! Save, work things out! Make…let me see…make soap from coconut, gasoline from cane juice, oil from cotton seeds, shoes from old Michelin tyres!' The war was very much here, just off the coast of Guadeloupe. Off shore, warships armed with machine guns ploughed their way through the Caribbean sea, tearing through the foam. The English, descendants of the legendary pirates revived for the occasion, raided the ships for merchandise coming from France. They seized cargoes of sugar, rum and bananas which were sent to the aid of our starving metropolis. Total blockade. So, the people from around here, who in times of peace already lived on meagre provisions, fell with their bellies on the ground into total starvation. It was the end to outdo all ends! We planted canes and bananas to supply the motherland and it was the English buccaneers who were eating at the expense of the French islands. We awaited, eyes glazed with hope, the arrival of supply ships. Hunger twisted our insides. The horizon remained empty. And the abundance of prayers was answered only in dreams, only there where make-believe feasts can swell your stomach and tempt your palate. In truth, the people around here did not find their generous France of yesteryear in this scoundrel of a governor who received his orders from an accomplice back in France and for whom we had to sing:

'Marshal, Marshal, Marshal
Marshal, here we are!
You have given us hope anew!
The Motherland shall be born again
Marshal, Marshal, here we are!'

Then, when General de Gaulle's voice filled the airwaves and rose to the heavens, the chosen ones recognised in him the words of a new saviour. They responded to the call in droves! They were dubbed dissidents. They left the shores of Guadeloupe, at night, travelling in fishermen's canoes. Taking care to avoid the patrols, they crossed the raging passage of Les Saintes. With a little luck, a few arrived at Portsmouth (Dominica), where the English friends of the man de Gaulle were awaiting them.

When the war came to an end, over there in France, the monuments to the war dead sprang up out of the earth in the same dazzling way as these banana trees today, over-fertilised, which eat their way through the Guadeloupean countryside.

II
Glory

When Léonce passed beside the little well-kept
garden where stood, eternally brave and staggering,
the bronze flag-bearer laid low by the ungodly enemy,
he removed his cap and, yet again, assumed a respectful
posture before the stone monument. As was his habit,
he set about reading the names of those who died in

battle on the other side of the sea. He had known them all. Children of the district with whom he once shared the same school bench. Jokers who named him KOCHI!...Provoking fellows, cowards, wastrels who were up to no good when he was breaking his back in the fields to make the yam come up nicely, who were off chasing skirts while he was preparing for marriage...And here it was, by some strange twist of fate, they were now glorified, mourned, decorated posthumously! And for as long as men shall live, their names would be engraved in the marble and the history of France and of the world.

In the first days of the resistance, Léonce was thirty years old. Quite naturally, he offered his body and soul to a group of young people ready for any sacrifice in order, they claimed, to gain respect and dignity. Everyone knew they were plotting with the English and were busy transporting to Dominica those who dreamed of giving their lives for France. Léonce was all prepared. Thanks to Ma Octavia's warning, Myrtha would be short of nothing; he had stocks to last five to six years of war. He wanted to leave immediately, test his strength, brave his destiny. The motherland was calling to her children. Poor battered mother, always so good to her colony.

On the first day of the resistance, Léonce was reminded of his club-foot because of the great pity which filled his companions' eyes. Immediately, his dreams of glory flew away. With his heart heavy, a bitter taste in his mouth and his stomach blocked by the dregs of resentment, he went away, humiliated for all time. Mechanically, he headed for the secret rum shop which defied the curfew in order to make money. He had never set foot in it, but he entered like a conquering hero come, as it were, to take possession of the place. At this time, soldiers of the *tirailleurs sénégalais* patrolled the town nightly, tracking down late-sleepers and those tempted by resistance. They did not joke. They were so black, it was said, at least blacker than people from these parts, that they melted into the dark and would suddenly emerge, their faces slit by a white murderous smile. You heard only their tough, leather boots crunch–crunch on the stony roadway, and then, suddenly, the terrible shriek of lead discharged into the belly of some bastard cousin taken up with the idea of freedom. Léonce pulled up a chair, sat down, alone. He placed the burden of his troubles on the table and his empty head in his hands. His eyes shone with a brilliant intensity. His heart beat wildly. And his club-foot tingled. If he had had the guts, that evening, he would have chopped it off with one machete blow, to get rid of his misfortune once and for all. But he thought he would create much worse difficulties for himself and chased away this wretched thought. Then the tiny provoking voice, which had fallen silent since his gift had been restored, spoke again. It manifested itself first in his belly, just as if his stomach was grumbling. Léonce listened.

'Ah! Ah! Ah! What did you think, Kochi? You have good luck, love and pickney…and you wanted glory to boot. Dumb brute! You have forgotten your name! Take the object that tortures you in your hand and you will realise that glory does not come close to fellows like you!' The voice chilled his insides, froze his brain, coughed to clear its throat and its breath was icy like the wind from a passing spirit: 'Learn this. You are a quarter of a man. You will be called Kochi for the rest of your days. Your future will henceforth be just like your walk: limping!'

Léonce ordered a shot of rum while the voice kept on repeating its grating refrain. 'Pity!' he moaned, letting the profane rum take the forbidden path into his insides.

'Your wounded pride led to your ruin, Léonce. Yet you were well aware that you were bringing about your destruction. Could you not have, quite simply, laughed at yourself?... But no, you needed GLORY! You saw yourself leaping into a canoe, sailing off on a calm sea, landing in Roseau, Dominica. You wanted excitement, heroic courage, primitive fear. You dreamed of a war wound, a medal, a cross of this, a stripe of that, a rank, gold braid, a knighthood, recognition for who you are. You wanted your name to echo throughout the colony. You longed for the prestige of a uniform, an army at attention, guns on their shoulders. Motherland, here are your children! And on seeing you, people would say: "That's him. Ninette's Léonce, the hero who went to war!" Must your life, in order to be fulfilled, necessarily go through these strategies, this fire, this spilt blood, this vanity?'

135

The more Léonce drank, the more he had the feeling that the rum gagged the wicked voice. So, one shot after another, he drank. All night. To the point of forgetting his Christian name. For a moment, the voice disappeared. The poor man thought he was safe. He rolled under the table and slept until early morning. As soon as he opened an eye, the voice was at him again, fierce, hoarse, vicious: 'Kochi! Kochi! Kochi! That's your name! You are not even a man and wanted to be a hero! Enough fooling around, my friend! Wake up from this long sleep and go back to your yams!' While the voice kept up its infernal taunting, one single thought ran through the fellow's head. He said to himself: My Lord! I am done for...! How will I continue to live with this shameful truth?

Up there, in the house on the hill, Myrtha waited up for him all night. A brass Pigeon lamp was burning on the table. The woman's eyes were awash in reflection, praying, wringing her hands, puzzled by every sound, by the stillness. Where had Léonce got to? He never went wandering around town, mixing with the folks down there. He had never spent a night far from his bed. When she thought of it, she remembered that he was behaving strangely that morning. He seemed to be looking for a light in her eyes; she had laughed. Then he went away without saying where he was going. Ah! she said to herself, this war has turned people upside down and made them crazy... She trembled, suddenly seeing, in a flicker of the lamp, the tall shadow of a *tirailleur sénégalais*. Lord

God, Léonce could be in agony, shot down by one of these black fellows from Africa. The hours slipped by like this, slowly, until morning.

The midday sun was up when, his clothes torn, our guy climbed on all fours the hill steep with his dashed hopes. His face was in a mess and tears had left trails of salt on his cheeks spiky with stubble. The voice went ahead of him, having a good laugh at his dishevelled state. Myrtha asked no questions and made no accusations. What was the point? He stank of rum. But, heaven be praised, he was safe and sound and she could not thank the Lord enough for this. She sent the children off to Ninette's and left him by himself, so that he could look like a human being again. That evening, he spent a long time sitting on his bottom on the veranda steps. What were the lights winking in the black heart of the town saying to him? What was he thinking about, poor fellow, banned from the paths of glory?... About a destiny of mediocrity... or else about the loss of his gift? On the day of Célestina's birth, Léonce had sworn never again to suck from the breast of rum. He remembered, too late now. And he was crying now, realising that he would never again see, nowhere in life, his granny Octavia. Would calamity rain down on his head from now on like the seven plagues of Egypt? When he slept with Myrtha that night, he felt he was really someone else, perfect, powerful, Myrtha's lover and not this cripple in whose skin he lived every day. His wife gave herself passionately to him, loved him in this new state and spent long with him. Alas nothing could get rid of the voice which now moaned like a virgin, now cackled with laughter as if playing a game of pulling wires.

Léonce wanted to prove to everyone, and most of all to himself, that the club-foot which prevented him from going on to the battlefields of France did not deprive him of life. So, during these years of scarcity, this time of Apocalypse, he worked hard on his land. You had to see him cleave the banana trees, cut the cane into joints, level the razor grass. Those who still remember the unleashing of this military campaign will tell you that the fellow laid low regiments of German soldiers with nothing but his machete. He decapitated them, chopped off arms and legs, slashed and slashed. His arm rose ha! and came down whap! His blows were merciless and his look was hard with the steel of guns and the lead from cannons. At that time, people called him: Marshal Kochi!, and spoke of his bellicose gardening like suffering worthy of honour... Is his pain he put in there! They didn't want to take him on because of his mash-up foot! Outside of this reality, the war went on far from the family. Léonce had stocked up on so much goods that one of the bedrooms was even changed into a storeroom. Their bellies did not cry out, oh no. But their heads, turgid like a ripe swelling, were engaged in contemplating a world where eggs could hatch only aborted dreams, dust-blown silences, water filthy with regret...

1955. It was now ten years since the war had ended. And each time Léonce stood before the monument

138

on which were inscribed the names of the glorious ones who died for France, this time of dishonour saddened his heart. He was only forty-three yet he was already taken for an old man. His hair was more white than black. At the end of the war, he cut his club-foot with a machete blow. From this time, his leg would not stop giving him hell. It inflicted suffering that gnawed down to the bone. Sometimes, especially in the rainy season when the nights are cool and the mornings laden with dew, he remained locked away, suffering in his room, turning and twisting like a worm. He could no longer walk without a cane. It was pitiful to see him, old, broken, staggering on his feet, on the arm of a Myrtha whose youth was still intact. Mercifully, the beautiful girl's feelings had not changed. She still saw in Léonce the ardent fellow dying of love for her, the same poet who once brought enchantment to her nights.

The day after his accident, Léonce lost for good the stability on which his reputation was built. The marvellous Garden of Eden produced nothing but sickly fruit. Every morning, at the crack of dawn, he still set off for the garden. But you knew that he didn't care. He waved the machete two-three times in the air, scraped away, as he went by, a tuft of guinea grass which told the story of his defeat, then he would give up, a beaten man. Leaning against the star-apple tree, he filled his head with the blessed days when the garden was not this field of battle, the time past when Ma Octavia looked out for him and appeared at any moment with advice, get up and go, or news…that time before the war. Eaten at by blight, the trees stretched out dead branches like the arms of drowning men. The birds no longer took the chance of nesting in them and flew by in the distance, frightened by the silence that reigned in that place. It was as if a great period of mourning had descended on his Eden of days gone by. When night fell on the hill, the trees became menacing, taking on the look of dishevelled ghosts, the shapes of monkeys, and crowded fiercely around our friend. Then he would shake off his apathy, grab his machete, which he wielded above his head, and, pursued by the ghosts of the evening, he ran and ran, breathless up to his cabin. His heart was racing wildly, but he would address his beloved wife: 'Ooooh! Myrtha!…You should see that! I have made progress today. Ah! Tomorrow…I will clear all the trees, plant yams, shovel and weed! Tomorrow for sure. You will see the beautiful fruit that your husband will give you!' And a laugh, more rusty than his old tools, made its way from behind his dreams. He resumed: 'You know, each day, I feel a little strength returning to me. I have not been in pain this little while!'

Myrtha listened to him, attentively, admiring his stubbornness, his drive, his courage. She knew that the wind of words, which knows neither ending nor beginning, was the last breath of air that kept Léonce in the hand of hope. So, she repeated after him, playing the same game:

'Yes, dear, tomorrow!…Tomorrow, the sun will rise

for you and you will do all that you have said. But now you must eat to ensure you have strength. Tomorrow will come sooner than you think.'

They sat down to eat in silence. The children said grace. And they swallowed their soup, their minds in disarray.

1955. Ten years after the war ended, Léonce had not noticed his children growing up. Since that tragic night spent in the pursuit of glory, he had not looked at them. He had not spoken to them. He had not listened to them. Célestina was about to turn twenty-one. Little Paul and Céluta had just become nineteen. Gerty was seventeen. That made it exactly twelve years that Myrtha had been raising them alone. Léonce believed that they could always eat from the reserves from the war. Alas, the stock of food exhausted and the garden now barren, sewing became the family's only source of income…

'One day for God, one day for the Devil!' said the townsfolk, dreaming of the time when gold was still prolific on the hillsides.

III
Célestina

Célestina had inherited her father's pleasing features: the smooth forehead, the same agreeable mouth which sometimes fell into the shape of her granny Ninette's unpleasant pout. Everything else came from her mother, especially her body, which revealed the contours of a country where hills swell discretely close to wild, abandoned coves...where the bare earth stretches on for ever and comes suddenly to dark mangroves.

Célestina once more cautiously pulled the straightening comb through her curly hair, which sizzled. From time to time, she cast a glance at her face, shiny with sweat, in the cracked mirror resting on the kitchen stove. If she listened to herself, she would have marked it with the hot comb. Out of anger and resentment. To punish it for being so beautiful. She trembled a little and burned her earlobe. She put the iron on the stove, waited a moment before picking it back up, wiped it on an old cloth and pulled it through a strand of hair. Why go to all this trouble, since she was more lonely than a one-eyed or hump-backed woman? Why break her back trying to straighten her hair in order to look less like a real black woman? she said to herself. Why follow all these different fashions whose only purpose was to please men, since she stammered horribly? The guys approached her, yes! as open as they were confident. But as soon as she opened her mouth, they had nothing more to say, were sorry they had made advances, and went off, their tails between their legs like whipped dogs. Handsome, ugly, bandy-legged and straight-legged, no-teeth and carnivore, Congo-black or mulatto-red, coolie, chabine, albino all fled, each in his own way, without even an 'excuse me, miss' sneaked between closed lips, without a little kiss. They couldn't stand the stammering which made a nightmare of each word, torn to shreds in such a pretty mouth.

However, Célestina remembered the happy days when she spoke like you and me. Then Mamma Myrtha sang in the kitchen. Papa Léonce chatted, told stories about his garden, brought home cartloads of roots, fruits and vegetables. When the family walked through the streets of Haute-Terre, the folks doffed their hats and greeted them respectfully. Célestina could see herself, ahead of the rest, with her brother and two sisters. She also recalled – it was in the middle of the war – how she began to stammer, for ever, when her father stopped talking to her, carrying her on his shoulders and, little by little, seeing her, as if she had become completely transparent. There were times when the girl felt she was nothing. Was she still flesh and blood? She must have fallen into some other dimension. A kind of void. One night she wanted to throw herself down to the bottom of the hill. But she thought of Ma Ninette, who had predicted the fires of passion for her, and she returned to the cabin where her parents slept. She was now twenty-one, she was furious and fed up of being stuck in this dreary spinsterhood. Célestina hated Haute-Terre, its deserted roads, its unfriendly humpbacked hills, its men with vacant stares, its doorways which protected the secrets of sleepy old bodies, with their toothless smiles from memories of passion long gone. She hated the young things who laughed at the sweet talk of the men, their hands on their hips. On evenings, weeping in her bed, the girl dreamed of a great love, of an accomplished man, with hair on his rough skin, a confident stride, the muscles of a body builder. She felt the embraces, the rapture and the heat. Right here, her life was an endless contemplation of despair. Elsewhere, her future would be written with nothing erased, she thought. To tell the truth, hope is a beautiful doll in a showcase... It was 5 July 1955. The following day she packed her belongings, got into a car and left, hair flying in the wind, for the bright lights of Pointe-à-Pitre.

Lucina had been living there for more than twenty years now. And almost as many years that she no longer put her foot in Haute-Terre unless it was in a pair of stiletto-heel shoes, whose height was in direct proportion with her dazzling ascent in society. Aunt Lucina was considered a fighting female. Although born with nothing to her name, she managed to make her way through life with all the trimmings. In her young days, Lucina did not dream of building a future in the shadow of some gentleman. She pictured herself on the highway of life, spurring on good fortune, snatching the green leaves of hope, setting fire to the underbrush of patience, riding on, riding on. She imagined herself as bird, flame, postage stamp, traveller's tree, spring and river, south wind and north wind. One day, after much begging, 'Can you imagine going all alone to Pointe-à-Pitre!', Ninette was obliged to give her, to see what fate had in store, a little money – enough to hold her for two to three months, enough time to get it into her skull that honest women suffer failure on this earth in order to remain with their families as long as a man does not come to ask for their hand. Lucina did not spend a penny of this precious treasure. As soon as she got there, she found herself a family of Italians who were looking for a servant. Sellers of eighteen–carat–gold jewellery, owners of a whole set of shops on Frebault Street, and lots of apartments legally rented, these people whined all day long, counting all the while the notes which they arranged in leather pouches, before stashing them deep in a secret container in the garret, or else depositing them in an account of the Caribbean General Bank. 'Aye! Aye! Aye! Life is hard for us! Taxes, credit! Aye! Aye! Aye! Here people don't buy gold like back in Italia! We are facing bankruptcy!' In fact, they were fat and prosperous, because the locals loved gold. Our Italians offered credit: 'We make it easy!' they said. 'You pay when you can, sweetie! Every month you come and pay down a little and in the end you will walk away with your gold.' The sweeties in question did not resist for long. They were wild about gold necklaces, pendants, fancy rings, heavy chains, rings studded with baccarat diamonds, rubies or amethysts. Then they would become indebted for years in order to wear the chains or the gold in whose name men had subdued the seas, conquered the land and spilt so much blood.

The Italians did not pay well, but Lucina had no expenses. She ate whenever she could, inherited dresses, shoes, hand–me–down bags and held on to her money. She cooked, washed, ironed, cleaned, waxed the floor and watched over the impotent grandfather, a schemer, who held a little cat on his knees, pretended to caress it and stuck his finger in its behind the live long day. The animal uttered feeble meows which turned on its master. And so one day, the kerchief in which she saved her pennies could no longer be knotted up. Lucina left Italy, her savings in her bosom. She wandered in the town for two days, her heart light, nose in the air, like a cat on the prowl. She covered all the roads. At that time, there were dangerous back–streets: meeting spots for gamblers; lanes that smelt of bread and sorcerer's incense; alleyways where coffins were carved out between barber and small shopkeeper; roads where cabins made of wood invited fires and concealed misery, women with fifty children, motherless men who drowned their sorrows in rum; the road of the Sisters of Saint Joseph, of the district officer, and of the loose women. La Pointe meant business. The shops, stalls and groceries sold a little of everything if you please, like in the heart of the countryside: a pound of onions from France, a gill of peas, one envelope, three matches, a scoop of lard, a pound of saltfish, two cloves of garlic, a candle...you trust it on credit! And you are off!

On the third day, Lucina stopped at the wharf. A steamer was offloading a group of American tourists while, on the other side of the road, a rather ugly house, all locked up, screamed FOR SALE, in white painted letters. Lucina had a kind of vision, the dream of a thriving restaurant. A mouth close by whispered the address of the lawyer who dealt with the matter. It was a run–down shop. The proprietress had just passed on and her heirs, 'all come off to something', whispered the blabbermouth, wished to get rid of this business which had fed them in childhood and paid for their studies in France. Lucina did not ask for all that.

Ambition sometimes gives wings to the passage of time. In some three months, the shop was transformed into a picturesque Creole restaurant that the owner named Exotic Delight. From the outset, no one confused this restaurant with the canteens in the market on which the exhausted dock workers would descend. The walls were too white. The tables boasted immaculate tablecloths – masterpieces of English embroidery – paid for in cash from the hands of higglers coming from Saint Lucia and Saint Thomas, and massive plants grew between the tables, climbed the shelves, came cascading down, creating a leafy ambience dense with a magical greenness. Paintings of naïve Haitian art hanging on the walls told the story of mythical worlds, of Gardens of Eden inhabited by a black Adam and Eve. The manager was also so beautiful, always decked out in lace and headscarves. Always ready with a smile, with a sweet word whispered in someone's ear, with the authentic way of laughing of a Creole lady of leisure. Very quickly, her graciousness, combined with the aroma from her cooking, attracted the important people, the bourgeois, the well-to-do, lawyers, doctors, judges, social climbers, businessmen...And naturally, landing from the cruise ships: American tourists! With their dollars and their amazingly pink, fat, hairy legs sticking out of wide chequered shorts. Lucina, in seventh heaven, flew from the kitchen to the counter, her feet light, a smile on her lips. Her guests always left with regret, their senses turned upside down. Some called her the magician. Others said she was the Trinity, three persons in one: cook, waitress and cashier. She smiled at these comments, knowing that the only miracles were sleeping in peace in the Holy Scriptures. She woke every day at three o'clock in the morning to scale her fish, boil her rice, peel her yam, beat her conch, shell her peas. She shopped in the markets, washed her tablecloths until nightfall in the basin in the yard and slept three hours, on the ground, in the dining room. No, it was not a question of magic, sorcery or miracles...only work and determination, around which were entwined the garlands of her creativity and the blooms of her secret recipes. At first they said she used evil herbs in order to captivate her customers. These rumours did not last because they were spread by people jealous of her know-how, mere cooks of ordinary food. She soon got to know all the influential people in the town. Its doctors, defenders and bankers all came to her. Out of notoriety was born respectability. She was invited to all kinds of ceremonies: legion of honour, wine of honour, prize of honour. She was welcomed in the town hall and the church. She knew all the sellers of gold, furniture and cloth in La Pointe, Syrians, Italians and Lebanese, who knew, like her, that the customer was a fickle child and business a wind that changes direction at any time. With business doing well, Lucina was not slow in using her money. At the end of ten years, she bought the house next door, had it demolished, built in its place a three-storey structure and set about renting out the apartments. Three cooks and five waitresses kept the restaurant going. The owner passed through every day at eleven o'clock, to put her secret touch to the food steaming in the pots. Lucina now said she was more Pointe-à-Pitre than Haute-Terre. And that she no longer had, I swear, much in common with those people with chapped heels, hollow bellies and empty heads from Haute-Terre. She urged Célestina to leave this neck of the woods where hope dragged around ball and chains on her feet.

1955. That year Célestina really believed that she would meet the man predicted by Grandma Ninette. Her aunt Lucina found her a modest job in a furniture store. I must tell you that because of her stammering – the girl had left school when she was twelve – she could not aspire to a better job. At last, Haute-Terre was behind her! That loathsome land where her life had become dreary between a father who had fallen into a great sleep and a poor mother worn out by sewing at night by candlelight. She no longer had any ties, not even her brother and her sisters, who laughed at her mangled speech. She especially hated the twins,

Paul and Céluta, the Devil incarnate as Ninette called them. Their wickedness knew no bounds. Already, in their childish laughter, you could hear the rasping of a diabolical soul. Later, when time came for their baptism, they had to be held in order to receive the sacrament. They screamed and fought so much and so well that the priest thought it wise to call Myrtha and advised two-three novenas to cleanse them. They grew up handsome and healthy but the hardness of their hearts was a bad sign. Around seven, while children all over ran off, fanatical in their faith, to Thursday's catechism, these two headed for the woods in order to torture lizards and little birds, before eating them without cooking or any preparation. At school, the children were terror-stricken when they saw them coming, so great was the reputation for wickedness that preceded them. Even the teachers, severe though they were at that time, never confronted them and, close to them, lowered eyes, voices, ruler, whip. The look of these two demons was as terrifying as the unbelievable stories which followed their every step. When he was eight, Paul, they said, killed his female teacher in prep school. Hiding behind a branch of white rayo, he flung a rock right into the middle of her head. The missile smashed the skull of the unfortunate woman, who was found not far from where she lived, skirts pulled up. Stuck in her immaculate underwear was a dead toad with gaping jaws. Her glasses had been savagely trampled. And her hand was down in a nest of red ants, where the letter

P gave away the guilty party. To this day, the law could not provide the final word to this mystery. P as in Paul, agreed! But you cannot accuse an eight-year-old because of a capital letter. Naturally, this crime shook all the Christian folks of Haute-Terre from top to bottom. Even though Myrtha swore on her life that Paul had come home just after school that day, no one believed her. The mother was trying her best, that was clear, but she could not handle them on her own. Caring about nothing except the frightening spectacle of his lost Eden, Léonce was not the iron hand in a velvet glove which their straightening out required. So, these children grew up more quickly than guinea grass, incredibly bad and phenomenally idle. Sometimes they disappeared for three days and then came back from separate directions. No questions were asked.

God be praised, thought Célestina, Gerty remained a little while longer by her mother's side. Gerty! Myrtha's last offspring. Her most beautiful creation. The one in whom beauty, goodwill and benevolence coexisted harmoniously. She had just been awarded her certificate and hoped to become a schoolteacher. She would soon go away. And that is how the family finally unravelled. The ties binding them together in the past had all become loosened with the hazards of the years. And even if Léonce and Myrtha tried each day to piece together their feelings from before the war, they knew, up there, that the word family was torn apart for ever.

IV
My Beautiful Friend

1965 found me on Schoelcher Road, the owner of a photo studio bought by my father, who died three months later in a road accident. The previous year, Mamma had passed on because of a chest complaint. I was an orphan and my only consolation was the thought of knowing that my parents were reunited in the good Lord's heaven. I had lost my crazy sense of humour, I had become serious, even a little rigid. I now owned property.

At first, the door, with its bell tinkled only on rare occasions: an emergency, the last hope for a passport promised as a special favour by a contact... 'The photographer who never has customers! It will be done quickly!' I spent my days waiting, looking invitingly at the clients who stopped in front of the portraits in my window case. But it is difficult to entice away customers from established people. I was even contemplating shutting up shop when, one day, a woman entered. An exceptional face, with a flat, open forehead above fine eyebrows, eyes like two onyx marbles, a small nose above a red, velvety mouth tinged with a hint of bitterness. More ingratiating than an old crafty Syrian selling on foot all over the countryside who scrimped and saved, I offered her my services. 'Would this be for a portrait, miss?' She gave a nod of assent. 'Do you want four copies?' She closed her eyes as if to say yes. 'I can offer you a small size...' She signalled no with her hand. 'Large size in that case!' She nodded. 'That will be twenty francs, miss, hum... which you will pay on delivery, of course.' She opened her handbag, took out a small purse made of pearls and counted out the notes, which she put down on my desk. While she posed, she did not say a word, merely smiled, winked, signalled her responses. Unprotesting, she followed my instructions closely. At the end of the session, she waved to me like an old acquaintance and went off whistling.

She presented herself the following day around ten o'clock. Then I understood her silence on the previous day. Her stammering broke my heart and my ears. There was a cry for help for each syllable saved. A hope dashed with each disembowelled word. A journey to the cross for her and for me, powerless to drag from her mouth the stubborn words which could be uttered only in agony. Every word that could be understood was a feat. And the smallest word that escaped safe and sound was paraded as if healed by a miracle. It was painful to witness the war that she waged, trapped in this disaster by God knows what ridiculous twist of fate. It was heroic seeing her manage, by stringing together, one behind the other, broken sounds in order to come up with some shaky sentences. The poor thing kept smiling regardless, pretending not to see me open my mouth awkwardly in order to prompt her to finish her words. The first prints delighted her. So she invited me to come, one evening, to dinner at her Aunt Lucina's restaurant, Exotic Delight, and on leaving, gave me her first name as a guarantee. Cécécélestina!

Time went by with still no customers. And then the owner of the famous restaurant, the still-beautiful Lucina – despite her fifty-five years – came next to pose. She was a small woman, sexy, affected, with ringlets on her forehead like Josephine Baker. In her eyes, outlined with mascara, I saw authority, ambition, power: burning orbs that sear the open grass and cleave in twain lesser mortals. (I have never been wrong in my reading of people's eyes.) Immediately, I resorted to my most skilful techniques. Retouched with Indian ink, her face took on a new quality, in which strength and softness faced each other in a fascinating struggle. I redrew her mouth, softened the severe lines that fixed it between parentheses and wiped out, with a stroke of the brush, the parallel wrinkles on her forehead. You must remember that at this time photography was in black and white. Nothing in common with the use of colour now, a poor reproduction of the original, a sad replica of faces devastated by lines, wrinkles, childhood acne, camouflaged by fat and other signs of ageing!...At that time, more so than my fellow practitioners in the square, I made over faces. I brightened dim eyes. I straightened nostrils. I put hair back on balding pates. I reduced or built up lips, without a scalpel or lancet. I was one of those photographers, I admit it shamelessly, who use faces as an excuse but are, really, interested in plumbing people's personalities. I wanted to become a portrait painter of the soul. To lay it bare. To scrape off the terrible shell deposited by the passage of time. To touch the essential self. And restore the timelessness that was there at the beginning...Huge project! My photographs were unique; products of my fanatical perfectionism and the hope, cherished by the model, of liking their appearance on the glazed paper...even if completely different, that which they could have had if time, fate, life had been a little kinder. I did not make

Lucina younger in order to win her favour. I was particularly fond of faces that had experienced half a century of life. Lined but not yet ruined. Her magnificent portrait hung, for twenty years, on the wall facing the main entrance, just behind the counter. She looked as if she was alive. Affable, welcoming, sweetly attentive to her clients, it inspired the waitresses, pushed them forward and shot arrows at those who dragged their feet and did not flash the kind of flirtatious Creole smile she had taught them. As the years went by, this portrait witnessed the parade of thousands of dishes, a good thirty styles and all the colours in creation. My fame grew because of this portrait. Soon my name was passed around by word of mouth. This is how I became a success.

Célestina was my first and last friend. My only friend. The beginning and end of the word friendship. I had got to know many people because of my profession. I had met throughout my life a number of interesting women and men, cultivated, touching, even sincere at times. In bunches, I had exchanged confidences and vows with quite likeable people whose last name, whose first name, whose face, I have now forgotten. Many have betrayed me, envied me and cursed me. I have hated them and then pardoned and forgotten them, because spite mixed with bitter memories gives birth to little monsters. I have journeyed, like a zombie stripped of its memory and which, in a thousand different places, looks for the memory of a former life secreted in the heart of impenetrable fragments. I have sworn fidelity, love, friendship, left and right, I admit it. At present, when I look back, I see masks tossed away after the carnival, powder and make-up, forced smiles... forced smiles. I have had only one friend: Célestina.

In 1965, when I first met her, Célestina was approaching thirty. I was twenty-three. She was beautiful. Alone. And more disabused than an old wounded donkey which transports the belongings of some homeless female. Célestina had a majestic bearing, but she stumbled over her life's hindrances, confined as she was in this prison of a tongue which had condemned and put in chains the dreams of her youth. When she had left the one road from Haute-Terre, with the attractive face of La Pointe smiling at her with all its false teeth, she thought she would turn her back, once and for all, on her unappetising life. Aunt Lucina was waiting for her. The Syrian was waiting too, with his gaudy furniture to be dusted. And maybe – who knows – the man that Grandma Ninette had predicted for her. Was he still searching for her among all the females who were chatting away and swaying their backsides in the heat of Pointe-à-Pitre?... Nine years she had been waiting! She sometimes imagined this mysterious lover. Black, but not too much. Wavy hair. A well-groomed moustache, soft to the touch. Starched shirt, stiff collar rising from a loose bow, fashionable suit. He would call her mademoiselle all the time. He would speak of marriage, partnership and pickney. He would be loving and polite, the replica of her papa Léonce, just before all this foolishness with the garden... Alas, hope is a stubborn creature... Célestina waited eight years in the dusty furniture store. Eight years of dressing up every day, of straightening her crinkly hair, making up her cheeks, polishing her nails, painting her lips, morning, noon and evening, in order to blind the males who floated by in the distance, inaccessible, on the other side of the show-case. They came in all right! Strutting, all smiles, chest high, with the half-closed eyes of those who have been condemned to the punishment of love. A smile was fine. But as soon as they wrung from her the first flirtatious words that Célestina scandalously massacred, they took to their heels, backing off in order to escape, they too stammering sorry excuses. In the evening, she cried about her loneliness to Aunt Lucina, who could not care less. She herself had married only business and money. In order to pull her niece out of her lovelorn desperation and to get her to forget men and their pricks, she initiated her into the art of cooking. Later, she confided to her the secret of her recipes, the till and the seven-headed key cast at Boulogne-Billancourt. Finally, in the presence of a lawyer, she named her her only heir.

Célestina came frequently to pose in my studio. That was her consolation, a kind of poultice placed on her distress. She loved to look at her impeccably silent face which concealed her stammering. Sometimes, she laughed at herself, saying she was a wordless beauty. A porcelain vase for display, with its flowered pattern and draped spider's webs of morning blue. Once she struck a pose, mouth wide open, tongue out stretching down to her chin. Her wet eyes belied her bitterness. Another day, she opened her heart to me. I remember it as if it were this very morning...one Sunday. We were playing a game of draughts. It was during the hot season when the sun has burned off the sky's covering and comes down to set houses on fire and scorch the living. One of those days when the air hangs heavily over La Pointe. Not a leaf quivers. Even the giant palm trees stand waiting for the stirring of birds. Sometimes an umbrella passes by but, at that time, the square is deserted. We were on the balcony of her apartment. As usual, she was losing. I was jubilant. When a silly laugh took hold of me, she gave up being patient and let fly a stream of spiteful remarks... That I was a real ass to sit there, with her, playing draughts on a beautiful Su–Sunday like that! That I did not have a man and that I would do well to hurry up and dig up one if I did not want to end up with a dog's life, with the loneliness of an old spinster locked up at home! That I would not be laughing for long if I–I knew beforehand of the sorrow to come! Suddenly, she fell silent, panting. Her words – bumping, stumbling, tototo, cacaca, dididi, hiccups – had come crashing down on me mixed with her tears. I was embarrassed and began to cry. At that moment, she ran her hand, long and beautiful, over my smeared cheeks in order to make me feel better. Then she related. Everything. Her blessed early years between father and mother. The hill with its fine promise. The secrets of her grandma Ninette. The coming of war like a disease. And Papa Léonce, who got up one fine morning without seeing her any more, without hearing her any more, without loving her any more. She had lost then the thread connecting words.

We resumed our game. A light wind made its way across the balcony, while clouds turned the red sky purple over the harbour.

V
An Ancient Curse

What I will soon tell you must, for ever, remain hidden away in a fold of your memory. Listen, but tell no one else! Hold your tongue! Sew up your lips tight with horsehair! If, one day, you begin to repeat this sad story, do not give either its source or its author. Know that I am telling this story in order to clarify things but, in my heart of hearts, I do not believe. This version of the story comes from Célestina.

Here goes. You have not forgotten Sosthène, Léonce's old papa. You remember the fellow's tragic downfall and then the miraculous cure from Ninette's fantastic hands and also the underwear washed in holy water which, shortly before the war, tamed the ancestor's wild ardour. OK, believe it or not, despite the hard times, Sosthène always found a means of procuring the holy water needed to wash his drawers! This is how he prepared, with his dignity restored, for his future heaven and exorcised that great evil that had poisoned a part of his life. Yes, no joking, you will agree that the moment is right to put evil back on centre stage...

When Célestina began to tell me her stories of evil, devils, sorcerers and Satan's followers, I had no desire to listen. I told her that it was that kind of nonsense that put black people behind like the balls of a pig. I urged her to open her eyes, tear away the veil, to abandon the well of superstition. I threatened her with ending our friendship. She leaped out of her chair, stammering that I understood nothing about the mysteries of life because I was born in town. We quarrelled, we threw extreme and harsh words at each other, we dug in our heels.

'You really think it natural that a man should suffer under such bondage? You–you think my poor grandfather was some kind of animal!' she let fly, chewing up her words.

'People are like that, that's all there is to it. He was simply more inclined to that thing. I think that...'

'In your opinion, bright spark! Can water alone, even if holy, cure someone's twisted nature? Use your brain! If a cu–urse had not been put on him, the holy water would have served no purpose! That's logical.'

'It's unthinkable that in this day and age people could be so ignorant!' I shouted, slamming my hand on the table.

'Poor you, you don't have a clue...Would the Almighty, through the intercession of Grandma Ninette, not have not ha–have done something if it was not a matter of the unspeakable one in person who raised in between all women Sosthène's spectacular weapon!' she declared, confident in her knowledge. 'Did this same demon not make these women blind, urge them to give in, impregnating them every time!'

'I'm leaving! I'm off! This is too much!' I would shout. I would get up, hurry down the steps and be right back up, to look for my bag, which I had supposedly forgotten. I would stand for a moment in the middle of the room and then sit back down, fascinated by her crazy stories, these disgusting tales and the attraction of omnipresent evil.

'Do you–you have a good nose for the scent of Satan at work?'

I told I did not want to hear any more. Then she filled my ears with the true story of her grandfather Sosthène. I made her to understand that I was not in the least bit interested in these stories, but she always had an answer for the logical and straightforward questions that I did not ask. She was absolutely convinced that all the misfortune inherited by her family resulted from bewitched water. Ma Ninette had repeatedly told her.

'When he fell over backwards, one fine day in 1966, Sosthène had lived twenty-five years of normal life (before taking advantage of his charm), twenty-five years of animal life (while he dragged around his infernal erection) and thirty-one years of living with holy water. It happened right there in church, just when he was picking up the offering from the assembled Christians for the projects of the priest, who, by the bucketful, blessed the water for his washing. Pa Sosthène collapsed suddenly, as if thunderstruck, and died without a murmur, his basket of coins in his hand. That spectacular departure loosened many a tongue…

'It was said that the three hundred thousandth collection would have been his downfall, after they found in his jacket a small notebook with a red cover. Since his redemption, the old man made a careful note of the receipts for every service. Such and such a Sunday: so much. Another one: so much. Palm Sunday: so much. Third Sunday after Easter: so much. And, on the day of his death – pure coincidence or deliberately planned – his notebook no longer had an empty line left. Could he have made a deal with God or the Devil, signing, with the end of the notebook, the completion of his own existence? You will agree, that explanation is a purely mathematical one...

'However, some who witnessed the spectacle had quite a different version. They had hauled his body over to the almond tree (the one providing shade for the large cross planted thirty feet from the church) and hurriedly took off his shirt and pants, to air out the fellow still warm but quite dead. They found underneath a pair of drawers. But what a state they were in! The material was rotten from too much washing and across the said drawers was draped a kind of eel. No one knew how it had got there. Women turned away their heads and bit their lips. A fellow who knew the deceased well, like everyone else around here, declared that the torn drawers had failed to act as a shield. Another thought out loud that Sosthène must have brandished his weapon one last time before being cut down by the poisonous air incompatible with his survival. You think that this must be the chemical explanation? Wait a minute!

'Others, who arrived in no time, swore that that morning Sosthène was slightly late and had dressed on the way, in order to avoid the priest's fire and brimstone. No! They were not old drawers that he wore that fatal day. Useless comments from women he had never checked! A new pair of drawers, yes! Brand new! It was an inauguration hiding that day under his Tergal pants. Ninette had bought them for him the day before, from a Syrian in La Pointe. As he had been advised, Sosthène, before putting them on, had immediately washed them in holy water and then put them out to dry on a rock in the yard. But that is where things went wrong... That Sunday morning, in his haste to put them on, he got tangled in the extra-long cord. So, can you imagine! By getting up and sitting down, kneeling down only to get up again in accordance with the pace of the hymns, the cord had little by little strangled the fellow's blessed penis and he did not dare in the house of the Lord to stick his hand in his pants to put everything back in its proper place. You hear that explanation which is derived from physics! OK, you can smile at these sordid figments of the imagination which have long made tongues wag in Haute-Terre. For here comes, my dear, the truth soaked in the spite of evil souls, those who make curses on their neighbours' heads, cultivators of killer plants, creators of misfortune, traffickers in deadly words and other purveyors of evil that Grandma Ninette fought in her time. I must now tell you a very sad story... that of a mother and her daughter.

'Marie-Josèphe, named thus in honour of the blessed parents of the living Lamb of God, was the fatherless treasure of a female from Pointe-Nègre who was nicknamed Five-finger-Nono. Nono's officially recorded name was Eleanor Machilbout. This nick-name went back to a time long past when a machete blow removed her right hand, clean! The shameful act of a drunken lover who, according to Nono, was not the real father of Marie-Josèphe. The rascal came out of her life with a spray of ammonia, full in the face, that blinded him on the spot. Marie-Josèphe was all of five when these troubles marked her mother's destiny. The girl recalled nothing of the wicked fellow, but she knew — because her entire childhood had unfolded with the single refrain — that men, even those with handsome faces and sweet words, concealed behind their masks ferocious dogs whose bites were merciless. Five-finger-Nono was certain that the whole breed of male lovers, more than any other, gave more trouble than Christ's crucifixion. The sin of the flesh, that's what had got her into trouble! So, she became fanatically religious, which allowed her to come to terms with her condition as a cripple, all the while harbouring deep within her an intense hatred of men in general. At the first discharge of blood from Marie-Josèphe, Nono went off to visit a well-known obeahwoman.

"'I do not wish for my Marie to live with anyone,'" she lamented.

"'That's a good thing! You should follow the sacraments!'"

"'I want you to block the fellows without honourable intentions. Let them circle my poor Marie! She must not be deflowered before first being blessed by the priest.'"

"'Well, fine!'" said the aged creature. "Bring her to me... tomorrow early, just before the cock crows. If it rains, if it drizzles, come back the following day, at the same time — the spirit I am invoking for this kind of job must not get his feet wet. Ah! I forgot... not a word to anyone until you return!"

'The following morning, with no sign of rain, mother and daughter, furnished with the bare necessities, knocked on the old obeahwoman's door.

'"Well, fine!" she muttered.

'The dawn visitors took their seats, side by side, on a bench of blackish wood, looking – through the corner of their eyes, their bottoms clenched – at the altar bristling with a profusion of burning tapers. A large cross threw a shadow across the room. The old crone began by burning a mixture of strange herbs which produced, in a flash, a thick foul-smelling smoke. The air became filthy with it. Nono, who had been buffeted the month before by a chest ailment, began to cough her heart out, while Marie-Josèphe cried and spat. Just like that, the old woman fell, full length, on the beaten earth of her cabin. She raised her face and set about screaming incantations in the language of the initiated. Five-finger-Nono held on with all her might to the bench, which moaned under her sodden behind, and resisted the diabolical spectacle. The same was not true for Marie-Josèphe. The poor girl staggered. Fell on her knees. And then collapsed while her eyes turned inside out.

'The girl awoke two days later in her mother's house. Her body was sore all over. Between her clenched thighs, a fire burned behind a macadam of wet leaves and smelly sulphur.

'"No vagabond will be able to pierce your virginity, unless he has first taken you to church," her mother whispered to her, with a kiss. "Trust me! After a while, you will no longer experience this pain. But beware!" She brandished her stump of a down–but–not–out soldier. "The old woman has warned me. There is a man – only one, God be praised! – who, fired up, can penetrate this defence…If, through some misfortune, this fellow crosses your path and slips into your body before sliding a ring on to your finger…I swear to you, if my name is Nono! for his entire life, he will pay for it. He will drag around until his dying breath a diabolical erection of which he will be a dumb-founded slave. Marie, my girl, no one knows that man's name or his face. Not even the wise creature who meets the spirits and traces with a raised hand the circle of Solomon. However, do not let this exception bother you. I think that this time the Lord is on our side. I want to believe that you will get married within the rules of the state and in the house of God. You see, my girl, I have told you everything. I have paid a lot for the old woman's work. You know why people have named me Five-finger-Nono!…He who has ears, let him hear! Truth and magic are with you. So come what may…"

'The old woman's magic worked. Marie-Josèphe turned off the fellows with dishonourable intentions who were taken with the arch of her back, the curve of her tits, the width of her hips and the splendour of her cocked bottom. No one was able to get close to her. There was always, between them and her, a kind of invisible screen, an unbreachable barrier, an

170

incorruptible paraclete...One tried to track her through the open ground in order to corner her behind a carrot mango tree. In a flash, the open land became a mangrove. So, he was no longer following in the steps of the beauty but sank down in muddy water and slime where crabs were running. Another one, close to feeling up her behind, collapsed, paralysed for a quarter of the rest of his days. During this everlasting period of time, doctors and obeahmen ate well because of his health. Yet another dived into a river where she was bathing. He swam and swam towards her. Sure of reaching her in four strokes. Ten strokes, twenty, thirty...he was suffocating. A hundred strokes...he sank like a stone. An impossible conquest, Marie-Josèphe gradually drifted away, like a mirage from the Sahara. Three fellows, a mulatto and two Indians, drowned in the effort to reach her. A madman attempted to serenade her under Nono's window. A thunderclap flattened him.

'When Sosthène made his appearance, in his prime at twenty-four (measuring one metre ninety-one, muscles on every inch of his body), Marie-Josèphe saw him no more than she saw the others who staggered, sank and drowned around her. Our boy claimed that, in all honesty, he would honourably slip the ring on to the girl's finger. But as sure as the fact that you do not buy your land without paper and witness, he wanted – before taking his oath before the law – to taste a little of the flesh which would take his name and the rest of his life. Was it such a great sin?

And what if he were to discover, after mayor and priest, that Marie-Josèphe was a lifeless virgin! He loved the beautiful girl from a distance, since to get close to her lay in the realm of the impossible. He opened his heart to a neighbour of earlier times, an old-timer with pipe and hair the colour of old hemp. They used to say that, in his time, he was reputed to be the most valiant cock within a hundred-league radius. Our hero always answered to the eloquent nickname Iron Wood, but that was pure presumption, a hangover from another life. Iron Wood gave the young Sosthène a vial that oozed an enchanted liquid – a clever mixture of ilang-ilang and three other leaves said to be secret – concocted on the island of Dominica.

'"Three drops for the wind that bears the seed. Three drops for the earth on which we feed. And, when you are in the vicinity of the girl, scatter also three drops behind each ear for the evil spirits, useless words and the glory of men. If you do as I say, you will get through," the old-timer assured him, his eyes glistening with a grotesque envy.

'Sosthène had taken off already. He scrambled up and slid down four hillsides. He walked and walked a long, long time, sniffing the path, the woods and the fields which exuded the vanilla perfume of the inaccessible Marie-Josèphe. Finally, he came upon her. At the edge of the river. Her back was turned. Sure of herself. Seated on a rock. Busy washing. Her bottom was magnificent; an anatomical treat! When he discovered this altar raised to the glory of love back or front, Sosthène almost broke down. Moved, spell-bound, fascinated, he hauled out the vial resting in his pocket, counted out three drops in the air, three drops on the earth and three drops behind each ear. And then he waited. Marie-Josèphe did not react immediately. But the way she was washing changed. First of all, she opened her thighs wider, as if to make herself more comfortable. Next, she began to rub the clothes at an incredible speed. Her entire body was taken up in this act. From behind, you would have said a boxer was massacring his adversary. Her shoulders rolled. Her bottom rose and fell on the overwhelmed rock. Then she began to sway like a drunken boat. Her assets took flight anew. Sosthène saw the ark of all his hopes struggling in the downpour God had visited on the earth. He was about to go to her assistance when she changed course. Scenting the smell of the male who could satisfy her senses, overcome by lust and her fiery heat, she rose and threw her dress in the river. Drunk, she staggered towards Sosthène, who, while blessing old Iron Wood's science, quickly stuffed the vial in his pocket. She fell into his arms, as if she were drowning. Sosthène revived her, you might say. Her protection collapsed with a gurgle which was anything but religious. Sosthène must have remained five hours in the poor girl's body. Five hours of digging the same foundation. Five hours to extinguish the fire whose leaping flames licked the belly and ravaged the hips of Marie-Josèphe. Five hours of an infernal yet divine clinch. Yes, he kept repeating, I will make a formal proposal to Ma Nono.

'"I will make a respectable woman of you, Marie, my love. But before, promise me!... What you have just given me, promise, swear! That no one else shall know that uncharted country. Tell me once again that I will be the only one to go along that particular way of the cross... The only man! Your pumpum is sweeter than coconut drops, more fiery than pepper sauce, deeper than a moonless night. You will be my sugar and my salt. You will be my sun, my sky, my earth. You will be my bed, my sheet, my pillow."

'They lay there, stretched out, one against the other. Their entwined feet beat the water lapping against the rocks. Marie-Josèphe lapped up Sosthène's crazy words, which described the future, built with the cement of love and the sand of great dreams.

'Alas, destiny had other plans in store. Close to the river with its clear water there stretched an open field of low curly grass. A woman was standing there. Five-finger-Nono in flesh and blood. Her arms raised to the heavens, she looked like a huge tree with its main branch removed. Her frame stood out, terrifying, in the encroaching dark of the night. Nono cursed the devil who had led this fellow to her Marie. This fellow had found the crack and overturned the canoe of hope in which her ruined life was placed. When her voice rose towards the heavens and then came back down, sharper than a machete above the lovers' heads, Sosthène realised that his life was about to enter a period of great disorder.

"May you be cursed, you rascal!
I, who they call Five-finger-Nono, will make you
    walk on all fours in the pigsty of sows.
You will beg for pity, you will beg for mercy.
You will have all the women you desire but none
    will love you.
You will be the slave of your long, fat prick.
And you will pray night and day to come out of
    your darkness.
I am going! And Marie-Josèphe is leaving too.
Do not try to stop her, never...
You are cursed!
Know that the day you see her again, at that very
    moment you will die!'"

Ma Ninette knew because all these facts had been
revealed to her by Sosthène himself, after she had
delivered him from his bewitched erection. That is
how she pardoned his roamings, his wanderings, his
women and his bastard children. Ninette was,
according to Célestina, the only one who could
explain the sudden death of her dear Sosthène.
According to her, on the last day of his life on earth,
the old lecher must have found himself, in the middle
of the church, face to face with...Marie-Josèphe! Yes,
that same virgin had been led by chance to come and
pray in the holy church of Haute-Terre. The poor
woman did not know that the man taking the
collection was the one and only fellow who, more

than half a century earlier, had lighted a fire in her belly and torn the veil of her innocence. At the time, Five-finger-Nono had not placed the curse in vain. At the very moment that Sosthène stared into the eyes of the old, ugly woman that Marie-Josèphe had become, the man's heart stopped beating, his blood stopped flowing in his veins and air no longer entered his body.

'Do you see the power of evil people! Do you now understand that evil is everywhere!' shouted Célestina.

I laughed at these tall tales and invented, in turn, an explanation for the old fellow's death. A heart attack seemed logical, more likely than these wild guesses. He was carrying a good age, his heart gave way. Célestina would not back down, going over, one by one, all the threads of the story. I was sulking in a corner, angry with myself. What was I doing there, having a discussion with this poor sick girl who always preferred a diabolical hypothesis!

'No, I swear to you,' she said, 'Pa Sosthène's death is not due to a numerical coincidence, nor to the age of his underwear, nor to the tightening of a new cord, nor even to a heart attack brought on by age…But really, make no mistake, to the coming to pass of an ancient curse.'

After that story, I avoided her for two weeks. I always had an excuse ready to decline her invitations to dinner. When she came to be photographed, I found an excuse in my work and my lack of time. She said nothing and went away, smiling like on the first day.

VI
Wise Words

Wise men say: misfortunes never happen singly…

The year 1966 is framed in black ink in Léonce's memory. Almost fifty-five years old, he did not expect anything good from the years to come. Time washed over him like rain on a dasheen leaf. Nevertheless, he did not anticipate any calamity like this one. They had barely committed Pa Sosthène to the earth when death was already on its way back to take away his mother.

Ninette, who in her time had cured with her miraculous hands a whole heap of people feasting at the banquet of misfortune, fell buddup! into the net cast by madness. After the last shovelful of earth had been thrown on her late husband, she continued for a short while to gulp down air mechanically. But life had lost its taste for her. Now that he was dead, she began to miss her old Sosthène. In the past, she had begged God and the Devil to take him back, so irritating was he with his old obsessions, his affairs with the females, his badly raised bastard pickney growing up in a desperate search for a father and feeding on the bitter milk of their manless mothers. She hated him because he had spoilt her youth, sucking out all the life in her and even her dreams and her secret places. When he fell into a depression, she did not stop chastising him, so that he too would learn what married life teaches. The day he told her of the spell put on him, Ninette believed everything. And then, she had her doubts. A hopeless liar, the dog had reached an age when men, even the most red-blooded male, are happy to sit back. Now that he was no longer, she wanted to know the reason for her tears. All alone in the cabin of miracles, she questioned the benevolent spirits who had come to her assistance so often. Bogged down in a mangrove of questions, chattering, singing, wasting away more quickly than a cheap candle, she passed away by the dry season of that same year.

Scientists maintain that there is something known as the law of series. I do not know who picks these wonderful cards. What is certain is Léonce was in mourning three times that year, because of Myrtha...She was just turning fifty. Still in perfect health. She could still even climb trees, better than a young girl! During the season, she picked a whole heap of breadfruits, oranges, avocados and limes that she sold in town. If, since the last war, she had not got going, the children would not have come of age. And Léonce, having become masterfully don't-care, promising each day a better tomorrow, would have undoubtedly drunk filthy water from the water jars and filled his stomach with air. Myrtha climbed into the breadfruit tree, fell and her neck broke crick! like a matchstick.

Folks with no future, no bread, nothing, who wander about these parts, their eyes wet with a sense of desolation, said among themselves: 'The more you down and out, the more old dog bite you!' Célestina, as for her, declared that it's an ill wind that blows no good...Orphan and widower in the same year, Léonce fell buddup! back into the hustle and bustle of the life led by everyone. This kind of catastrophe completely flattens you or else slaps you back to life. He forgot clean about the grief that his impossible Eden had brought him. And here is how healing came to the supposedly incurable wound which, for years, contaminated his existence. So one morning, he was seen, dressed in black, digging a deep hole ten feet from his cabin. Without anger or bitterness he threw in his machete, his hoe, his pickaxe, his rake, his two shovels, all his old digging companions. It was as if he was freeing himself from the chains that had bound his soul ever since the loss of the gift. Soon, the weeds that he had controlled around the house began to multiply like a family of rats. A high, dense forest took over the garden, which had known, in times gone by: perfect furrows, proud trellises, cherished fruits, pruned trees, weeding, planting, cutting, trimming...Léonce decided to put it all behind him, to forget it like the first communion he tasted the day of his renunciation. And even if the grass grew in thick rows all around and the hill sprouted rasta locks to drive him crazy and frighten the folks down below, not a furrow wrinkled his brow. He no longer had any battles to fight. Death stretched out its stick to him. Sometimes, the evil voice piped up from deep in his bowels and spewed a bitter bile into his heart. He would haul out his flask and pour himself a shot of aged rum. What was preventing him from drowning in that liquid since he had become an outcast? Already, before he lost his wife, as soon as the sun left its place in the sky, he spent nights seated on the veranda steps or else slumped in his rocker, finding pleasure in sipping defiantly from his chalice. Quite often, the stars illuminated his fifty years of life. His thoughts went left and right and he saw everything...Ma Octavia, who had deprived him of his gift because of a bout of drunkenness, his children, who had grown up so quickly and already gone away, his Myrtha, taken away by destiny. He counted the branching stars, followed with his finger the curve of the moon veiled like a blind man's eye. He cocked his ear to hear the love song of the toads, imagining in the warmth of her resting place the broken body of his Myrtha. His only visits were full of shame, asking her to excuse the feelings that overcame him in the early morning before Brother Sleep crushed him with one blow in the light of day.

When her grandmother died, Célestina and I were no longer that friendly. I refused all her invitations. For her part, she only rarely darkened the doorway of my studio, leaving me to myself. Her eyes were often wet, filled with so whys. We exchanged moments of long silence, empty glances, lame words. Her stories of curses, evil spells and other kinds of magic had driven me into those directions where logic and reason together set fire to tales of sorcery. I was suddenly in demand, required on the Leeward Side today and demanded over in Saint François tomorrow. I did not show reluctance when it came to work. That year, a wild idea kept occurring to me: to change my whereabouts, to leave the ancient wooden cabin where I started in order to locate myself in a concrete building. Far from Exotic Delights, very far from Célestina's neighbourhood and all the zombies that followed her around. I was not therefore seen at the funeral of her grandmother Ninette, the very one who had taught her to question the dead and feel attached to obeah. I nevertheless sent her a message of condolence, just to satisfy my proper upbringing.

Even today, I regret not attending Ninette's funeral. That day, I lost for ever the opportunity of seeing Myrtha. Excuse me! I did not know, I swear! that Célestina's own mother was that very Myrtha that old Barnabé had told me about, the so-called genuine mother. I would have run. I would have scrambled up hillsides if things had been better explained to me. Put yourself in my place! Is it that real life is constructed according to this pattern of coincidences that is retailed in folktales! Is it that chance has a habit of shaping stories like these!

Célestina was in tears when she announced her mamma's death. The 23 October 1966. I will never forget that day...She was wearing a gingham dress buttoned up wrong. Her hair, normally pulled together in an austere bun, was held by pins stuck in any old way. She stammered the news to me while collapsing into a chair. I consoled her a bit, saying I was with her in her grief. 'But, it's a pity, I cannot, even with the best will in the world, attend the funeral...If it were today! But tomorrow, I am busy all day. See you soon. And walk good, take care!...' With these words, I showed her out, my arm around her shoulders the way hypocrites do. The following morning I turned on the radio, rather out of habit. The gloomy music of the death announcements suddenly filled my bedroom. And the words began to fall bup bup bup!

Like coconuts being picked…We regret to announce the death, in her fiftieth year, of Mrs Myrtha D…née B…daughter of Boniface B…and Mérinés G…wife of Léonce D…leaving children: Célestina, Paul, Céluta and Gerty…Families…relatives and friends… the funeral will be held on…at the church of Haute…I was holding in my hand a picture of my mother which I was about to put down on my night table. One moment later, out of the blue whence came the news, I do not know why I was walking on broken glass and my foot was bleeding. With these two names juxtaposed – Myrtha and Boniface – the scales fell from my eyes, the doors opened wide, the day dawned. Look! I am still trembling to simply think of that ridiculous day. They had said Myrtha and Boniface, but I had heard Mirna and Barnabé… Célestina, my neighbour, my friend for a while, was the direct descendant of the Barnabé I met one idle day, when I was seventeen. I absolutely had to attend this funeral, on my knees, with my feet bleeding. I was thinking that Barnabé had perhaps put Célestina on to me so that I would locate Mirna. I had not understood or rather so late. However, I was the only one who knew. The only one to put the pieces together. I would have told Myrtha about her real mother, Barnabé, the real name she got at baptism. I would have told her the story of her old father, Archibald, the torment of passion, the ways of chance…Pulling myself together, I closed my studio hurriedly and rushed off to the Exotic Delights. Lucina was already settled in the back seat of her Mercedes, her short driver was adjusting the rear-view mirror and Célestina was getting in.

'Wait for me! Wait! Please...I am coming!... Please...I am coming with you!' Tears were streaming down my cheeks. Lucina made a little sign to the young man. I ran back home to pull on, without ironing, a black taffeta dress smelling to high heaven of camphor balls, and dashed into the street, my heart in my mouth.

'Thanks,' said Célestina without stammering, squeezing my hands too tightly.

During the journey, I did not say a word. Célestina was crying into a handkerchief. Lucina powdered her nose several times. The cane fields slipped by outside the car window. What did this Myrtha look like? I had dreamed of her so often. Because of the two-three words from old Barnabé, a number of images came to me. Sometimes, without summoning them, they came in a great rush and flooded my mind. I was following Myrtha-Mirna to Boniface's funeral, walking alone towards an already foretold destiny...At her wedding reception, I was dancing somewhere. She, innocent and loved, queen for a day, was holding Léonce's hand, seeking assurances for the future. Wearing a crown of orange blossoms and lost in a dress of satin and lace, she was waiting for that one moment of happiness. I saw her also climbing hills, a bucket of water on her head, bringing lunch for Léonce, who was planting the garden, calling out to the strange woman who haunted the hillside, giving birth to and feeding her children, sewing, washing, ironing, and then, seated in the middle of her cabin, gazing at her dreams as they fell away like a kite cut loose.

When I finally saw her, dead flesh lying in a white pine coffin, I began to cry again. I recognised Léonce by his club-foot. He stood in a corner, an old man broken before his time. Lips pinched, he seemed to be listening to something being whispered from a great distance. On his right, Gerty, the schoolteacher, was delicately blowing her nose. Paul and Céluta were talking outside, on a bench, accompanying the stories they were reeling off with wild kicks. I was the only one crying, even uttering sobs and the muffled moans of restrained grief. People began to stare at me. The older ones especially who had known the deceased in her prime and did not manage to put a name to my face. They muttered things like, 'Who is that?' 'Where the lady come from?' 'Must be some distant family of Myrtha from Grande-Terre.' Disturbed by the whispers, Léonce raised his head. He looked me up and down like a cold wind which instantly dried up my tears and my display of emotion.

Stuck in a corner of the house, I tried to make myself invisible. What had got into me! I was making a spectacle of myself. My eyes were red and swollen. How to explain my tears? I did not know the woman. I was a stranger. I should get the hell out of there as soon as possible... Suddenly, realising that I regretted not having brought my camera, a nauseous feeling of shame overcame me. My eyes could see only through a viewfinder. My profession had corrupted me. I was a despicable creature, a stealer of privacy, preying on images and expressions. Just one exposure after another. Always, until I got fed up!...Family portraits in happiness and in grief, death, life, no matter...teeth exposed, or tears, whatever you prefer...I heard the click, click of my old Rolex, click, click! click, click!...What was I doing there since there was nothing left to see? Since Mirna was dead...Yes, I would have shot it all, loaded my camera and fired it off at everyone without stopping, the people gathered, the dead woman, the gloom and the grief. I gave a little wave of goodbye to Célestina and went away, head lowered, muttering 'excuse me' as I made my way out. But I did not count on Léonce. You should have seen him! Standing stiffly, at the entrance to the cemetery, his cane pointed towards me, barring my exit. I could have gone back but our eyes had met. 'Where are you from? Who sent you here, at this time when everything is coming to an end? You are crying and sobbing for whom, why? Tell me, who are you, so choked up with grief? You are in deep mourning! Is it your mother that was just buried? Whose family are you? Tell me your name and that of your relatives! Reply!' he ordered, hitting the pavement with his cane. I backed away a few steps, stammering four or five incoherent words. Already we were surrounded by several people, those who loved a fight. Célestina saved me by entering the circle. She put her arm around my shoulders and Léonce put away his cane.

'Ah! She is with you! Bring her to me one of these days! Bring her to the hill! I would need to chat with her a little…'

Much time has passed since that day, washing away sadness and regret. Almost twenty years. Today when I come to review things and put them in order, I do not know how many times I climbed the hill of this Mr Léonce. I listened for long hours to his stories broken up in the waters of memory. I got to know Myrtha and Ma Octavia, the famous grandmother who died and came back, the inspired prophetess who disappeared for all time. I witnessed the lives of Sosthène and Ninette, his late parents. I cried just once when he said to me, 'But that is not your concern!' I laughed a lot too, up there, because you must laugh at your own misfortunes in order to have the strength to follow the path that leads through unknown woods. I asked questions again and again in order to see how the threads of times past were unravelled.

VII
Paul, Romaine and Céluta

When Paul hung around her neighbourhood, Célestina became pale and lost all energy. A chill ran down her back. Her ears rang. Her nostrils began to quiver. And her heart beat as if the end was nigh. Célestina said that Paul was no ordinary mortal. A diabolical soul rumbled within him. His eyes glinted behind a childlike face. His classic mouth with its generous contours was terrifying because of the meanness of his features. At any moment you feared it would open and spit out tongues of flames. Célestina told me of the cruelty he made her endure, in the time before her departure from La Pointe; I stood there puzzled for a long time. When she brought up the schoolteacher struck down by a rock and swore to me that her own brother, Paul, was the perpetrator of this murder, I did not believe what she was telling me. Célestina saw evil everywhere. I had already observed that... If she had twisted her ankle leaving the restaurant, if a bird had sung in this spot at a given time, if a coin had fallen next to the till and rolled into a crack in the floor, if a spot had appeared on her right cheek, if a fly had landed on a lobster bisque, if a crease had persisted after ironing, if 14 July was celebrated on a Friday, if a loaf was eaten by rats on a Monday... Célestina pointed to spirits, evildoers, zombies, sorcerers, Voodoo priests from Haiti, old-timers' magic and black mass. Evil was inscribed in each flickering moment of existence, in every shudder, in the slightest sigh. She had been raised in the shadow of her grand-mother Ninette, who kept showing her the evidence and the manifestation of evil. Ninette was the source, the beginning of all her beliefs. She taught her the powers of vials of coloured water which make dreams come true and enslave the beloved, revealed to her the scent of good spirits in a ray of light, whispered to her magical refrains which suck out the juice from their marrow and dry up wicked people. She described the monkey-like contortions which bring good fortune and love and life in the hereafter. Ninette lay with her an entire night so that she could breathe in the same breath and sweat in the same fluid. She sucked her finger, stuck her with a golden needle, mixed her fresh blood with a golden coin found in the shadow of a goose's feather. She made her swallow a gram of mercury to protect her from poisoning and dunked her in countless baths with beneficial powers. After the death of her grandmother, Célestina found herself with no one to lean on. So, she began to consult obeahmen in the countryside, who hide their activities in houses painted blue. Because she had been trained to give mystical explanations to everything, she could not resist this temptation. When her mother died, I gave up speaking logic and reason to her. I no longer challenged her beliefs. I simply listened to her, curious about these tales that opened extraordinary pathways for me...

So here is Paul's story according to Célestina... She said that after hurricanes and earthquakes, her brother was considered the third calamity that threatened Haute-Terre. After he left the hill when he was twenty, people breathed a sigh of relief. They thought he had taken off for good. Alas! he came back. Every year, he was around. He always returned, worse than a wound from obeah. When they saw, far far off, the outline of his unmistakable silhouette — he had inherited his grandfather Sosthène's massive stature —

Literature humanizes you.

people melted into the darkness of their cabins. After three – four signs of the hooked cross, the Christians kept asking the Almighty to protect their bodies and their possessions. Young virgins were locked away deep in the huts. The fowl coops were barricaded. They let out the watch dogs. You could say a curfew was declared.

What did Paul live on while wandering through the byways of Guadeloupe? Célestina could not say for sure. Nevertheless, she could always describe, as if she had witnessed them herself, the abominable crimes perpetrated wherever the fellow showed his face. When he reappeared in Haute-Terre, panic struck the devout souls. They said that gold coins found their way unassisted into his pockets. He had only to push his hand in. They said he shook a money tree every Good Friday. Someone said he had seen him on the wharf of Basse-Terre where his prostitutes worked. The rumour circulated that he had been to jail. That he had made a fortune in Venezuela after discovering a gold mine. That his business went from strength to strength because of the workings of a Voodoo priestess from Haiti. They also claimed his money came from a deal with the Devil and that his spit was poison...

As soon as he got to Haute-Terre, Paul went and placed his bottom on a stool in the old bar run by Ma Rénel (don't ask for any more information, it is two years now that she has passed on because of a stroke). He pulled over a bottle and drank straight from it. And then he threw some coins on the floor. Simply for the pleasure of looking at the woman's fat lumpy behind, searching for pennies in the cracks of the flooring. Suddenly, the bar fell silent. The fellows sipped their punch with renewed vigour, stopped sharing out cards and slamming down dominoes. Mouths, like fish caught in a net, gulped air without uttering a sound. You could hear the flies buzzing zoom zoom zoom. Serlise Rénel became soaked with sweat and wiped her brow with an old rag. At this point, Paul jumped up like a spring in a mattress picked up in the dumping ground and, worse than a hurricane, descended on the poor woman. He dropped some big kicks on her behind. He laughed, she groaned. He screamed, she asked for mercy. The customers became like transparent paper–thin silk, deaf, dumb, blind and crippled. Hats were crammed down on heads. Heads were squeezed down between shoulders. And the shoulders hatched the egg of cowardice which says this is not my business!...Don't get me involved in these things! Not one of these proud rumsters, everlasting boasters, would have got up to help the black woman. They said that, at some time, these two had indulged in pleasure together. So, it's none of my business!...When Ma Rénel had received her share of blows, Paul offered a round of drinks to celebrate his return. The fellows straightened up and words resumed their coming and going between the tables. A game of dominoes came to an end. They turned to playing cards. Paul said goodbye to the fellows, blew a kiss to Sérlise and made his exit, leaving behind the echo of his loud laugh, which filled for a long time the ears of the men gathered there.

Paul then went off to visit his uncle and godfather, Hector. It was a ritual that everyone knew. What Hector called his house had been built over the ruins of Ma Octavia's cabin. He had extended it and improvised with no concern for aesthetics, throwing up, left, right and centre, some so-called rooms made from old, roughly dressed planks. The whole structure was covered with a patchwork of zinc combining the new and the rusted, retrieved from the dump at the Saint-Eugénie plantation. Hector claimed to be an official cutter, meaning: cane cutter. Out of season, he spent his time at sea, fishing. He was now father of six sons and two daughters. For a few pennies, his wife, Agathe, ironed clothes for people. Hector worked without much enthusiasm. Without killing himself! he said. To what end? For glory! For wealth! These two women who, for so many years, had strung Léonce along… What was the point of praying, storing up, cursing and blessing? What was the point of envying and loving, since you are sure to become, one fine day, a meal for worms which crawl about under the earth, for ants that run about in bones? And to end up, end up like the lowest of animals… So Hector did not show his face to God, the Devil or man. In the mid-afternoon, you could stumble on him, seated under a mango tree in his yard, meditating. Meditating on life. Chewing his old pipe. Meditating. At this time, Hector was the only person who did not fear Paul. Because of this, no doubt, his nephew respected him. This big scamp did not greet or hail anyone besides his uncle Hector. As big as he was, he still kissed him, continuing a gesture of politeness learned in childhood. When he asked what news there was, Hector pulled out his pipe, responding with a few banalities on life and death, then turned to him and asked:

'So, what about your journeys! Where did you get to this time? Do people die the same way everywhere on the earth? What is life? Tell me, my friend...What is life? One long, useless torment, not true!'

'Godfather, you think too much!' said Paul, laughing arrogantly.

'No, it's a long time since I have finished with meditation. Now, I understand things fully. Look there at these mad ants! Look closely and you will see men, women, the rich, the poor, blacks, mulattos, whites... How to separate them, by colour and money?...Now, pick up one of them at random. Yes, it is in your power! Do like death. Have fun. Crush it between your thumb and index finger. Ah! You see, you see...'

Often at this point in the discussion, Paul dug around in his pocket in order to fish up some money. A wallet appeared immediately. He pulled out notes, one at a time, one at a time, like a magician out of a hat. At the same time, Aunt Agathe appeared in the doorway. She began to complain: 'The children have not had a piece of meat to eat these days! School is expensive and so are shoes! Raymonde needs a new dress!' And without further ado, she leaped in, grabbed the notes without saying good evening to Paul and disappeared into a room, shaking with a hearty laugh. After a short while, shouts and comforting sounds followed. The children begged, 'Yes, Mamma! Oh, yes!' Agathe promised this and that, while outside, Hector was showing Paul the uselessness of paper money and the value of wisdom.

'Have you found wisdom, my son? Wisdom...'

'I did not seek out wise men, Godfather! Is money I look for, is money I find!'

In his twenty-eighth year, Paul decided to stop travelling. The news made the rounds in Haute-Terre in no time. Fear took hold of people like a bout of diarrhoea. They were not prepared. You could see, the following day, fine, upstanding people packing up house and pickney. They were going away never to return, escaping a future of terror that was promised by the definitive return of Paul, the tormentor. Others, equally worthy, suddenly undertook major projects they were putting off until tomorrow for the longest while. That is how the very first blocks of the town were laid. The bravest ones simply placed a bar across their doors. A few began to grease their guns furiously, sizing up how many bullets were left.

So Paul came back to live in Haute-Terre. But this time he was not alone. He had in tow a tiny white, or maybe quadroon, woman, all bones, without tits or backside. She walked three steps behind him, looking straight ahead. To summon her, he whistled or grumbled something that she alone understood. One day, it was learned that the girl's first name was Romaine. Little to go by but this discovery opened new possibilities... With such a name, perhaps she came from Italy? Did they still sell slaves over there? Someone from the war who had travelled ventured that she must be the victim of the white slave trade... Did Paul buy her with his gold? When asked, a schoolteacher contradicted this story and suggested her origin might be in Grande-Terre and the mixing of albino and Matignon white. Rosette Méliard's neighbour remembered that her grandmother told her the story of a slave... 'A poor black woman who had the same name... Her masters had made her see hell and its damnation. It could well be the same one who came back to take revenge for times past.' Whatever it was, though she was white, the woman called Romaine worked like a black female. Paul had appropriated the piece of good land that his father had acquired in 1937. He built an ugly house on it with wood and zinc (despite his spectacular hoard of money, he did not use blocks... no one knew why this was so). Romaine loved the garden, the animals, the river. By seeing her come and go, they got used to her. She was not someone who carried much weight, but she had in her something that compelled you to respect her, to take her seriously. She was generous and freely gave away portions of her crops. She spoke little with the rest of the neighbourhood but they knew nevertheless that she came from an old family. Paul had found her planning to go to France. Her family said she was good for nothing, except for serving people whiter than herself. The boat trip was already paid for, the song 'Goodbye Scarves…' on the tip of the tongue. But Romaine was afraid of long voyages. As cursed as he was, Paul saved her from this exile. He said he would marry her and so she followed him. In fact, he brought her to Haute-Terre to eat the bread of misery. The poor woman did not complain, no sir. Perhaps, had she gone away, her funeral would have been announced a long time ago and her bones buried. Sometimes, he beat her. She did not cry out. A moment later, they could be found gazing into each other's eyes, not saying a word. And then they went into the cabin and closed all the doors. That is how they had their two children: France and Prospère.

According to Célestina, Paul had settled on the piece of land without even asking his father's permission. Gerty had tried to bring legal proceedings against him to obtain a fair division. Who did he think he was, this Paul! She would set the law on him! She would make him quit in a hurry! It was his lookout if he had not been to school! She had her certificate and knew all the provisions of the law!… Alas, word never became deed. Célestina reminded her younger sister of the incident with the schoolteacher murdered by a blow from a stone and Gerty ceased pursuing her rights and made the sign of the cross on her mouth.

Paul did not mix with those two. He could get along only with Céluta, his twin sister. She too had very early taken the road to independence, selling at one point her body and her insides on the wharf at Basse-Terre. Sailors, travellers, wifeless fellows, Indians with no flesh on them had their way with her, one after the other. It was her way. Already, before her departure, they swore that with Paul (her own brother!) she lived like husband and wife. More than once, they had come up upon them, their bodies entwined. When they left the town, the remnants of a burned-down cabin provided shelter. It was after the death of her mother, Myrtha, perhaps a whole two years later, that Céluta came back to Haute-Terre. She pulled out of her blouse a wad of notes that had nestled snugly in her bosom, counted up her fortune and went off to see a certain Détonnère, a carpenter by trade. That is how she came to leave the port and its pleasures and settle down thirty feet from Paul's cabin, on her father's land. In front of her house, Céluta threw up a shed, a few stools, rough-hewn tables on which she arranged glasses and bottles of rum on a tin tray. At that very instant, her bar came into being.

VIII
The Conspiracy of the Past

'Be careful!' Célestina told me one day, 'do not judge them too harshly...Before pointing your finger, always try to understand how past events are interwoven. All I have said to you is true. No, I have invented nothing: Paul and Céluta are truly cursed. Unrepentant creatures! Damned souls guilty of mortal sin! They have given me a hard time, you know...But today, even if you do not see me mixing with them, I have forgiven them in my heart.' I raised an eyebrow, anticipating that she was going to rattle off one of her stories in which devils played the main roles. She crinkled her nose and began to stammer out this story, which I had never heard anywhere...

'There once lived in Haute-Terre a young girl without father or mother and raised by her old godmother. Her name was Mona. Poor girl, one ill-fated day, she crossed the path of Grandpapa Sosthène. It was during the period of his curse. She fell under his spell, lay down with him without hesitation, spread open her thighs and got her due. Alas, after fooling around, like all the others who had gone before, Mona saw the man of a hundred thousand spells vanish. Mona was fifteen. The year after, fate put her and her fat baby in front of the church where Sosthène was getting married. She almost lost her sight. She staggered and stumbled. The crowd parted and she collapsed while the married couple gave each other a kiss of love for their lives together. They carried the girl to her godmother. The baby cried for a long time in the arms of an Indian woman who had been with Sosthène in the past and was now raising his bastard, the product of chance, bad luck and sorcery. Sosthène was marrying his beloved, the only one he had not managed to penetrate. Of what had taken place, he heard nothing, neither screams nor tears...nothing but the heavy breathing of the crowd. He did not recognise Mona. He saw nothing, except – perhaps – a few women's faces, with their strange, disturbing black eyes. Mona had not disclosed to anyone the name of the father of her Emmanuel. Not even to her good godmother, Floria, who was raising her according to a strict Christian education and who would have sworn before any priest that her goddaughter had never known a man. For her, this child was surely the result of the work of the Holy Spirit. The sanctimonious old woman died in ignorance in 1954. And Mona, who could read and write, found in the town hall a position in the Registrar General's office. Despite her fatherless child, everyone respected her. Especially because she possessed a knowledge that everyone held in high regard in this country which is searching for its history lost in the depths of the dark days of slavery, on a boat from Colombo, in memories of Brittany or what is left of the memory of someone a hundred years old. Mona knew how to find her way back through family trees. She spent nights gently turning the tattered pages of old registers. She wore out her eyes deciphering the names and dates written in an extravagant hand by municipal employees who died in the previous century. That is how she forced Sosthène's ancestors out of the dark and became so passionately interested in his descendants.

'Emmanuel, her son, was growing up nicely. Each Sunday, Mona was on the verge of telling him: "Look at that man there! The one with a Bible covered in white paper in his hands. You see that tall fellow on the arm of the woman wearing a hat with feathers. That gentleman is your papa!" But she swallowed her words instead of blurting them out once and for all. Pulling herself together, she dismissed thoughts of Sosthène and concentrated on listening to the Scriptures, the homily and the sermon. Each Sunday, her heart was filled with a little more bile. Her mouth became bitter. An unmitigated hatred rose from her insides and within her emaciated body her soul burned red hot. The girl did not visit obeahman nor sorcerer nor fixer-man, but this persistent fury that she exuded needed to be cured. When her boy turned five, Mona began to invoke the Holy Spirit. She was weary of fighting this evil that became worse each Sunday as soon as she caught sight of her impregnator.

'Someone whispered and told her that favours asked of the highest saint were granted without exception. So she tried. Who could blame her? She simply wanted justice, enough to cause five or six generations of Sosthène's descendants to tremble...

'When Ninette's belly showed promise of a first birth, Mona found consolation. She begged the Holy Spirit to do everything so that the fruit of this consummated marriage would be packed with seeds, infested with worms and that its future should have neither rhyme nor reason, just like those people with nothing who fight with dogs over bones. Try to imagine the infernal pleasure that made this wretched woman's flesh tingle. She thought herself all-powerful

202

and even close to God because she kept company with the Holy Ghost, manoeuvring her enemies like puppets of wood and string. She saw herself as the sword of justice because she prayed in front of tapers blessed by the priest. Time rushed by. The first wrinkles appeared followed by an accompaniment of white hair. When she was forty, because she had breathed in each day the stench of evil, Mona lost the attraction of her youth. She prayed fervently on the head of Léonce, who, poor fellow, knew nothing. Alas! Despite his deformity, the fellow walked upright. When she looked at her Emmanuel, Mona could not make head or tail of life. Her beloved child, her one and only, in whom she had placed all her hopes, who had turned into a man now – already twenty-four – had become an idler, dedicating his life to rum drinking... Then, Mona asked herself, perhaps if he had known his father, Emmanuel would not have sought out the company of shiftless and lawless rascals. The same ones who waste their time in games of gambling, cards and dominoes and endlessly drink rum that makes men brothers and clouds their tomorrows. Perhaps if Sosthène had married her, Mona, instead of that worthless Étiennette, her Emmanuel could have been this young man who without reproach and without fear married in 1933 a certain Miss Myrtha. On Léonce's wedding day, Mona abandoned her prayers to the Holy Spirit and directly called upon the forces of evil. Who could cast the stone at him? she said to herself. Her Emmanuel had become embittered. And all that was Sosthène's fault! Therefore this Léonce, who was awash in too much happiness, had to pay for his share of the tribulations inflicted by his renegade father.

'What did she have to lose at forty something? Her life!...Her life was a string of disappointments. Her soul!...Since Sosthène had brought her down, her soul was drowned in the blood of her lost virginity. Her Emmanuel!...She saw him only between bouts of weeping. Alcohol had made her poor son so dissolute that Mona lost her mind. She no longer had anything to lose. After her nights of sacrilegious incantations, she said to herself that the Lord would be able to answer her pitiful prayers.

'O Mona! Wha–wha–what have you done to my father, Léonce?' Célestina stammered, raising her eyes to the heavens. 'The poor innocent did not know either the date or the time of his birth, when Grand-father Sosthène (already cursed by Five-finger-Nono) impregnated you in the woods; wha–what have you done because of hatred and jealousy, Mona? You have planted a diabolical weapon in Papa's groin... You have condemned his offspring because your Emmanuel was depravity incarnate. A reject who whispered to you, "Me love you mamma!" with rum on his breath. Wha–wha–what did you ask of the evil spirits? O Mona, I was too beautiful for your liking, eh! So, you sent such a frightening spirit to confront me that a never-ending stammering took hold of me that very instant. You are the reason I am lonely today.

Your thirst for vengeance is insatiable, Mona!...You can never have enough. After that, you suffocated in my mother's insides the boy who was coming. And then you put the twins into the very hands of Lucifer...Alas, you did not know that by delivering them both, you were making a deal; in the kingdom of darkness, two children's lives are worth a young male's soul. That is why on the very day when Paul and Céluta's cries rose above the church's choir by the baptismal font, your son, Emmanuel, perished in flames, inside a filthy hut in which he lived at the edge of town...

'I have already spoken to you about the ruins of the burned cabin. It was there that the twins came to have fun in the middle of the rats. You see how it is all linked, how destiny plays its hand. Do not believe that the earth on which we blindly walk is dumb...Look at how alpha and omega are always connected. That hut was the very place where Emmanuel, his body ravaged by alcohol, collapsed. Sometimes he did not have the strength to get there. He would collapse at the roadside and only come to his senses when men were heading out to the fields. He did not remember either his name or his mother's name, nor how he had landed in a ditch of vomit.

'24 August 1936, baptism day for the twins, the one Emmanuel hardly drank more than usual. His body stumbled, however, like an old cart on a rocky road. The sun was stinging high in the sky. And then, suddenly, it disappeared behind a grey cloud. Shadows entered by the open door. Emmanuel shuddered. A cold draught, impossible in this part of the world, made his ears stand on end and froze his blood. He got hold of a lantern, poured the gas on the canvas and struck a match. The flame leaped up at the very instant. For a long time he watched it burning. We will never know in what far-off places his thoughts wandered in these final moments. Furthermore, we will never know why, all of a sudden, a great tiredness sucked away his energy. Our man crashed on his bed of rags, settling the lantern like a docile woman beside him. The cabin burned down. And with it, the pitiful fellow who befriended rum and made his mother weep every day. The hut was consumed by itself! Without scorching the slightest tuft of grass around there. It burned with no one as witness and the fire died with no smoke, with no 'Fire! Help!' No one saw the fire. People could do no more than confirm it. The forces of the law turned up with Mona. She recognised here a charred tibia, a skull with lumps and rotten teeth, there an unidentified bone or the remains of a scorched hip bone. They threw the remains of the victim in an old saltfish box for her. Tears were shed in the cemetery. Mona dropped out of sight until the day when, in agony (it was two days before she died), she came to prostrate herself at the feet of my father, Léonce, in order to... Guess what! Confess her sins and beg his pardon. She was afraid of not going to heaven! Well, this was how all got to know who was the father of her dearly departed Emmanuel. How her diabolical dealings and her murderous prayers were spread out in public. How we measured the extent of the bad luck inherited by Léonce and his descendants.'

IX
Shadows are but Faces

In 1970, the year in which Papa de Gaulle left this world, Gerty, Myrtha's last child, celebrated her thirty-third birthday. Ever since her first day as a schoolmistress in the elementary school, her life had right away taken the direction of order and discipline. At thirty-three, Gerty was no longer seen as a young girl. Without really noticing, she had become an old maid with her obsessions, her quirks, her solitary pleasures, her afternoons spent embroidering and her annoyances. Although she retained for a long time her slim twenty-year-old figure, time had deprived her of the bloom of youth. She lived alone in a big concrete house built on land bought with her savings. Marriage! Gerty did not want to think of it. However, men swarmed around her. She received, you could say, proposals morning, noon and night. Alas, she never found one that suited her. Nothing but idiots! Stupid! Goats! who were after her possessions. 'Get married!' she laughed. 'You mean submit to some man's control!' Use her breasts to feed a bunch of noisy children. Peel vegetables. Wash underwear. Scour out pots and pans. And wait for him to return from his adventures. Hope for his return. Pray that some rival was not already pregnant. Pray to the Virgin Mary so that some female would not take her to an obeahman... The mere thought of such a gloomy future made her nauseous. Célestina would babble: 'Ho-how can you reject love when it comes knocking at your door? Hurry up and grab one of them before your hair turns white!' Gerty had better things to do. She read. She educated herself. She cultivated herself. The fate of Woman was a challenge to her. She had just finished *The Feminine Mystique* by Betty Friedan and now followed, with special attention, the gains of the Feminist Movement. She even exchanged a few letters, dense and brief correspondence, with a group of militant French women led by Christine Rochefort and Monique Witting. When you got to know her better, she relaxed a bit and you had a chance to get to know the great passion of her existence. A famous poet dominated her life. He was the companion her heart desired. He never raised his voice except on paper. When evening came, by the light of a cosy lamp, he whispered soft words to her, perfuming her nights with rare scents taken from the heart of divine verses that she leafed through dreamily as soon as the falling dusk enveloped the naked sky.

There came a time when Gerty set foot in La Pointe only to visit the library. They ordered for her by air the reprints of the works of Mr Hugo. She knew the life, the personality and the style of this giant as if, at each moment of his existence, she had been there, to hold the candle, clarify the thought, listen to his first reading and be thrilled with happiness. More than the novels, poetry read out loud, at night, gave her such pleasure that she rose the next morning, dripping with sweat and out of breath. Only a hot basil tea could break the spell of his *Voix Intérieures*, his *Chants du Crépuscule*, his *Rayons, Ombres, Contemplations* and also his *Légende des Siècles*. At the time, they said that Gerty put Hugo above her Creator, that's what ruined her. As she made her way through his works, the scales fell from her eyes. Evidence and theory were verified one after the other. One day, she was overwhelmed by this realisation: Hugo was truly the new prophet, the unheeded visionary whose divinely inspired writings guided blind mankind towards the Word. Hugo knew and took into account the existence of spirits. As for spirits, they were a dime a dozen all over the earth, binding the hands of men of goodwill and snaring hope in this country clogged with evil! They swarmed around in the twilight, entering women's bodies, flying from tree to tree and walking at night on the zinc roofs of houses. Good and evil struggled with each other all day on the roads of Haute-Terre. Hugo had seen them, like Ma Ninette, who so often struggled and eventually overcame them all. In page after page, Gerty found responses to fundamental questions of life and better understood the darkness of this world. Hugo was a great prophet who had not been sufficiently blessed... 'Yes, thanks to these thinkers and these wise men/The Shadows are but faces/The Silence is filled with voices!' she repeated, in a state of ecstasy, tears springing from a land from which reason has fled, flowing softly down her cheeks, sunken because of sleepless nights.

In November of the year 1970, Gerty, her mother's most beautiful creation, drifted into a quiet, romantic lunacy. She was removed from her position as schoolmistress and sent off to the asylum. Five years of confinement did not put a stop to her mania. As she was clearly not dangerous, she was handed over to her family. One day in 1975, she alighted from a taxi on the arm of her papa Léonce. She had really changed, the poor thing. Her furrowed face looked like the cracked walls of her house. Her hair, which she used to hold in place with a banana clip, was now grey and cut short. All skin and bones, she could be taken for a mosquito with long, black, frail legs. No one knew why her sister Céluta took her in. Although, to be honest, after Mona's death, the wickedness of the twins became less frightening. Perhaps because of the confession and the repentance of the woman who sinned ... The errors of youth were now put to rest in a past that no one cared to revisit. In 1975, Céluta's first shed had given way to a huge upstairs house built by the grace of rum. Downstairs was taken up by a new bar where males from the neighbourhood met. And the wives continued to curse Céluta, calling her a shameless whore who turned men's heads by scandalously exposing her titties, which poured out of her forever unbuttoned blouse. Paul came each day to have a drink or two at his sister's. He was now the father of two children and terrified only one or two hypocrites. In 1967, France was born. 'The most beautiful girl in Creation!' said Paul, who had travelled and knew the beauties of France and that country's fame throughout the world. Two years later, Romaine gave birth to a boy named Prospère, so that he should never lack possessions. Haute-Terre realised that this wretched Paul could no longer be that evil when they saw him taking the little ones for a walk and buying ice cream. He walked with his head high and his gaze fixed in the distance. His eyes twinkled with laughter sometimes. Thus the years of mystery and crime that piled up behind him were automatically placed on the head of Mona, Satan's devotee.

It was thanks to Céluta, Paul and Romaine that Gerty did not die in the year of her return to Haute-Terre. The first sent her food every day with France and Prospère, who were taught to read and write by the poor mad woman using passages from *La Légende des Siècles* and *Les Contemplations*. Paul, the only one able to make her take her medicine, took her every month to visit a doctor who treated mental illnesses. The rest of the time, she was left to drift through her delirium, which she maintained like a marvellous garden where poetry and prose bloomed like wild flowers.

One day, I went with Célestina to visit Gerty. Célestina got it into her head to send her on a trip. Someone had told her that Haiti was the last resort. Over there they knew how to cure this kind of illness. A photo was needed for the passport. Gerty smiled on seeing me. I do not know if she recognised me. Her sister took her off to a bedroom to fix her hair and put on make-up. I remained alone in the drawing room looking at books wildly scattered on the ground, photographs of Victor Hugo torn from literary magazines, rough outlines of poems, sheets of paper, folded, torn, illegible scribbles. Before sitting still for the portrait, Gerty asked me to pay attention for one moment and began to declaim these few verses:

'I picked this flower on the hill for you
 On the sheer cliff overlooking the sea,

That the eagle alone knows and alone can approach,
The shadow bathed the sides of the gloomy headland;
I saw just as one raises at the site of victory
A great triumphal arch in shining gold,
On the spot where the sun had sunk,
The sombre night build an entrance of clouds.'

Célestina gave up her travel plans. I do not know why she asked me to destroy the pictures of her sister. Today, I do not regret having kept all the prints, which I will show you in time.

X
France and Prospère

One day, Célestina told me that Paul enjoyed a kind of reprieve but that he was still prone to terrible seizures that were obscure in origin. During these attacks, the wickedness of the past disfigured his face. From his eyes flames leaped, while out of his mouth gushed an inexcusable language. When the moon was right, his body, possessed by a devil, lost its senses. Arms and legs were twisted tight just like mangrove roots. Drooling from the corners of his mouth, he was thrown to the ground, his limbs uncoordinated. In these moments, the wretched man did not recognise his family. 'You simply,' said Célestina, 'had to wait for the spirit to leave his body.'

I remember his daughter, France, when she was five or six years old and climbed her grandfather's hill every day. She was a brave little girl. Léonce called out to her all the time like a nervous parent. 'Fwans! Watch out for the guinea grass! They can cut worse than a barber's razor! Fwans, you will break your neck, come down from the tree now for now! Ay, Fwans! Stop shaking the guava tree branches! There are honey bees everywhere!' When she grew up, Léonce complained that he no longer saw her. He said that now she had bubbies pushing through her blouse, she preferred to remain in town and drive the young boys wild. I met France again in 1976, the year when Soufrière spat its ashes on Basse-Terre. The authorities ordered an exodus when, in the middle of the day, night threw her great black sheet on the green hills. I had just crossed all of Grande-Terre, travelling in the opposite direction from the people fleeing the lava, the ash and the promise of a destiny identical to that of the people of Sainte-Pierre in Martinique, slain in the eruption of Mount Pelée in 1902. Feverishly, I photographed the cabins being rescued on carts, people on foot, weary, driven towards an unknown salvation, pickney crying, old-timers still dazed from having to leave chickens, pigs, home, belongings. I reloaded the Leica I then had twenty times, immortalising the crawling automobiles, draped with mattresses, suitcases and old, rusted trunks. Nothing must be lost. I had to catch everything: the anxious faces, the laughing children, the scarves tied in haste, the fear, the horror, the policemen and the soldiers, the firemen, the goats set free running about in lost herds, ropes still on their necks...

When I got to Haute-Terre (which had not been declared off limits), I found Léonce in a state of great excitement. His eyes blazing, his hand cupped around an ear stuck to the radio, he was jubilant:

'It will blow up! Boom, boom, bodomboom! Like the German bombs on the heads of the French during the war! Boom, boom! And all Guadeloupe will disappear! Let's get it over with...! Ah! It's you, my dear,' he said, seeing me. 'Put your things down here. What do you have to say? Have you been following this bacchanal since the beginning? This morning, you had to see them! A parade of mad fellows, caca from fear in their drawers. Magma is what they call them, those people.' He burst out laughing.

I was crushed. I was suddenly discovering a loath-some creature. I had loved him so much until this day. He had become the grandfather I never had and I shared with him my stories of love and grief. He always showed a great wisdom, an infinite goodness. Good God, I had come upon a family from hell whose members wore masks behind which were concealed diabolical souls, a world of wickedness, sanctuaries for madness, fountains of lies, contempt and wrongdoing that made my heart sick. I was preparing to take my leave once and for all when France entered, shouting:

'Granpa! Granpa! It's Aunt Céluta who sent me. She wants you…'

'Take off your hat in this house and say good morning to our friend before shouting like that!'

'Good morning, good morning!' France said impatiently, throwing her hat on the table. She did not kiss me, did not even look in my direction. She was now nine but looked like twelve. Very tall. An unformed beauty. With a look that seemed to have lost sight of the shoreline of youth. 'Aunt Céluta is telling you that her bar is full of poor unfortunate people who do not know where to go. There is weeping and wailing in there. They are looking for somewhere for them to stay. Soufrière will soon explode. They have lost everything. They have left their…'

'Eh heh! Ah so! Is it me who must suffer in the place of these sinners!' Léonce grumbled. 'And if it was really the end of the world, eh! Would Céluta call me then too…? With all the sins she has to her credit, I could do nothing for her! What can I do, tell me? I must stick my finger where the Almighty has put down his own hand! Or else take my cane and drag my sixty-four years down to the open land to listen to their lamentations! She can just share out some rum, that will warm them inside!' He laughed at his way with words and, his face twisted by a malevolent smile, stuck his ear once more to the radio.

Upset, France turned to me for support. But I was at even more of a loss myself. I did not know that Léonce who got so much fun from other people's misfortune. Why did I always have to invent for myself perfect friends, pictures of negatives that swirled through my brain? Why could I not bear to see them different from the first impression they gave of themselves? Incorrigible idealist that I was, I was always disappointed by the new sides they revealed afterwards. That is something I sought in vain in my lovers and friends: perfection! Uncompromising perfection that prevented me from accepting others as they were. Unattainable perfection that made me react with disgust if they departed in the slightest from my ideal image... An image sealed in laminated paper, as with my photographs. That is where I was in my thoughts, when France spoke again, pleading with the old man:

'Granpa! Listen to me! You are alone in this house. You well know it is too big for you. You have a whole lot of rooms locked up! Take in at least one family! They will pay rent. Think of the little children...' Suddenly, her tone changed as if a terrible thought had just occurred to her. 'I hate you! You are nothing but a mad old man! You spend your time telling your sorry life's story to this woman. You don't see that she is stealing your thoughts. She makes you enter her camera and, little by little, you surrender yourself totally. She does not care about your stories! One day, we shall see your photo in a book on the Antilles which will travel the entire world. You will be there, seated in your rocker, with your cane, your twisted foot and your hat. The caption will read: An old-timer from Guadeloupe. Not one more word. And that will be all of you, your life, one point, that's all, all that defines you!...So, go ahead and pose for the photographs! You think you are special because the lady from La Pointe climbs up here! Your heart is dry in truth and your brain gone...'

Léonce started. His hand clenched his cane. He shook his head three times and gestured with his chin to show that France had won. She could bring people, he would accommodate them.

At fifteen, France already measured almost one metre seventy-five. She batted her eyelashes constantly, revealing how much she had been assured she would be beautiful. She landed in Pointe-à-Pitre with, on her face, the look of someone who knows she was expected, entered my photo studio, demanded that I take her picture and so I did. Incredibly photogenic, France posed, pouted her lips, laughed for the flash, showing her perfect teeth, slightly parted, which added to her charm. Of course, she did not pay me. I did not complain; it was a real pleasure to photograph her. One evening, when we were dining at the Exotic Delight, France declared:

'I am entering the Miss Guadeloupe contest!'

A long silence followed.

'Yo-yo-you have already told your father?' inquired Célestina, who already saw Paul succumbing to a nervous breakdown.

'I will tell him only if I win!' France shot back, smiling slyly.

'Naturally! Yo-yo-you will have to if your picture appears on the front p-page of the newspaper! Your papa will skin you alive!'

Célestina was wrong. The day France's photo covered page one of a thousand and one copies of *France-Antilles*, Paul's happiness knew no bounds. It was because of the name she had that his daughter was famous, like France, he said, with a silly grin. He had predicted it. The following year she flew off to Paris. Everyone swore she would gain wealth untold with nothing but her personal charm – acquired at God knows what price, philosophical souls hastened to add. Today, France models for the great fashion houses. At first, she sent postcards from New York, Tokyo and London. She now limits herself to telephone calls always made from overly noisy airport lounges. Sometimes, we see her in women's magazines, her small pointed breasts draped in voile, her navel exposed, her legs on display, a huge head of hair sweeping her shoulders. 'We see her everywhere except in Guadeloupe,' sighed Célestina.

While France was spreading her wings, was her brother Prospère becoming wealthy? Do the names we give to children really influence their future?

Alas, Prospère was not prospering! Perhaps France one day took from her younger brother his fair share of prosperity... Paul himself understood nothing in this whole affair. His daughter shone on five continents and prosperity (which was Paul's doing) followed her closely like the tail of a shooting star... They said she earned millions by simply lifting an eyelash. The people of Haute-Terre, who were very proud of her, thought that evil had been done to Paul and that the obeahman had to be consulted to undo the spell. Célestina was in total agreement with them.

As a child, however, Prospère had, written on his forehead, the greatest promise. When beautiful France wrote illegibly and left the pages of her school books dog-eared, he was the object of praise from his teachers. Everyone said he walked at a steady pace towards his future. Alas, after finishing first form, Prospère took to visiting his aunt Gerty, Hugo's mad lady. That was the year when everything turned upside down. At first, Paul thought it could only help; a schoolteacher, even a loony one, had teaching in her blood! And his son, in his wisdom, would be able to take advantage of this. Alas, soon he would converse only with books, bringing them back from his aunt Gerty's ten at a time. Gerty encouraged him without completely leaving the meditative state, now permanent, in which she would forever live. Often Prospère stayed to observe her. She seemed perfectly happy to him, reciting throughout the day the huge

Légende des Siècles. Nothing seemed to disturb her, nothing distracted her, not even the sunlight and the shadows, marking the passage of time, which came and went by the jalousie windows. Prospère opened the old books with excitement and foreboding. What treasures did they conceal? What mysteries? What powers? Where would they lead him? How far could he follow those beings that he summoned back to life? By reviving their pasts did he not risk falling into the same hopeless mess as his poor aunt? At times, the words took on strange and dangerous forms, just like the dead brought back to life. He had only to blow on the pages to summon to life a drifting of spirits. On the eve of his fifteenth birthday, Prospère declared that he would no longer set foot on the road to school. Romaine begged him in vain. But Paul, who had left school at eleven, found nothing wrong in this sudden withdrawal. If Prospère did not take the road to fortune armed with the light of school diplomas... well, Paul said to himself, the desired fortune would rise from the earth, fields and bananas, especially bananas which were sent to France. There was no mystery, you had to plant! That was the future. Bananas promised money, loans and subsidies, progress, modernisation, yes! Everyone could see that the sugar factories were being closed one after the other. You had to accept reality, Paul said to himself: the future of Guadeloupe lay in bananas!...

Alas, Prospère did not have what it takes to be a cultivator of bananas. The vision of those extended fields, with their rows of future banana trees, leaves drooping, full bunches and flowers upright, brought to mind a deep sense of unease, the whiff of a past not quite put away, a feeling to vomit. In each banana tree, he saw ebony wood, a soul in agony rising from another century, a spirit rooted in this earth, imprisoned for all time. Terrified, he realised one day that the banana plantations were fields of slaves imploring the strongest of the gods in the universe to send a great wind which would take them back to the land of their ancestors. Fields of lamentation. Fields of tears. Sea of dread. Never–ending stirrings and noises. Where did these nightmares come from?

Prospère sat down behind the piles of used tyres in the storeroom of the service station where he had been working for a short while. He drew out of his shirt a newspaper folded in four and opened it carefully. The pages were soaked in his sweat, in his odour. He liked that. He smiled mechanically at France, who covered the the entire first page, then began to recite the text he knew by heart: '...Again this year, a rare flower bloomed in the closing hours of a merciless battle in which those vying for the title, outdoing each other in gracefulness, unveiled their charms and demonstrated, if there was need to, that the cannons of beauty can bring you to your knees as surely as our army's artillery. The audience, turning up in their numbers, proved once more its attachment to this noble pageant. Although a small fight broke out after the declaration of the results, the spectators could applaud at their leisure the new queen, who is named France. Her vital statistics leave you breathless: 87-58-90. A dream in flesh and blood! A warning to would-be suitors! France will do very well: a return ticket Pointe-à-Pitre/Paris; a cheque for a thousand francs offered by the S.I.N. group of companies; a dress from the house of Créolinou-Couture, located at 245, Road of the Last Runaways; a pair of shoes of her choice from Sarah Shoes, 78C, Schoelcher Street; a full beauty treatment from Orthensia International Black Beauty, 48, Henry IV Street. We wager that our new queen will be able to appreciate these wonderful gifts and bring honour to Guadeloupe, which she will soon represent at the contest for Miss France!'

Prospère folded the newspaper and left the store-room dragging the old pair of Mikas that he had on his feet. He had to patch a mountain of inner tubes and the manager would cuss him out again if he did not repair at least half in the morning. It was now a full six months that he was doing odd jobs as an attendant-handyman in this station. Fill petrol pumps, count cash, verify cheques, give change, measure the oil, wash cars, wipe off the windscreen, put air in the tyres, sweep and cut the grass verge. Prospère had no other ambition. A monstrous convulsion shook Paul when the would-be source of prosperity for the family stood before him and announced that the world of agriculture would have to do without his services. The banana fields that were springing up everywhere were plantations of ghosts, said Prospère.

One day, brought back to life by bad fertiliser, these evil spirits would shackle those that formerly had them in chains. Prospère refused to be an accomplice in these fields of the dead. He finished off his father by declaring that, in his eyes, nothing was as beautiful as the sight of a field of stars on the night of a full moon. Hugo sickness! thought Paul, who saw each day its symptoms in his sister Gerty. That's why, if you meet Paul, you never know!...After two-three polite words, ask him to explain these tribulations to you...Then he will tell you, with a conspiratorial look, that the worst obeahman in all of Haute-Terre was called Hugo. Wherever his books went, the prospect of fame and prosperity remained forever elusive.

Prospère walked by the empty office, pulled up a stool marked with an old oil stain and sat down, in the shade, between the two pumps. Not a car in sight. The one and only petrol station in Haute-Terre was the kind you see in those American series on French television. Blazing sun, dust on the deserted road and, from time to time, a lost car which drives up and disturbs the attendant, woozy from one beer too many...No! Prospère did not drink! He smoked. Prospère did not smoke cigarettes like Job, Gauloises, Camel or Cow-Boy on his horse. No, Prospère drew on what is smoked by pursuers of dreams, philosophers of the herb, desperate seekers for inspiration, creators of new worlds. Prospère smoked the herb! In secret...it was found out very late. He continued to look well and had his hair properly combed. He would go to La Pointe once a week. He always brought back books. No one realised he also ran errands in the ghetto. But where could one domesticate this herb of destruction in a place like Haute-Terre where, without trying too hard, eyes see what is meant to be locked away, ears hear words uttered behind closed blinds, or nostrils open wide like funnels are always at work, ready to catch, breathe in and identify the smells of dead and living alike, the odour of oil of stay-home, the stink of a chamberpot left open, the whiff of the dead returned to visit, the lotion of a she-devil on the evening of a carnival fête, a broth made from snapper, the smell of adultery, the scent of Rasta tobacco...? Usually, a secret buried in Haute-Terre immediately began to sprout, put out leaves in two days and quite quickly grew into a miraculous tree whose fruits were formed into a string of words to be exchanged with the first person to come by. Some say you must not cast stones at these people. They are members of the same family, products of the same hardships, heirs to the very same history marked by shadows and grief. They envy each other, scorn each other, love each other and seek out each other. Alas, if it was known that Prospère, instead of prospering on the road to the future, climbed his grandpa Léonce's hill...If he had been seen smoking herb, sprawled in his hammock, suspended between heaven and earth, in the middle of the cursed garden bristling with bush...Perhaps the secret would have come out with the first whiff of smoke and Prospère would have been saved...

I remember him, last year. It was the rainy season. A bad cold kept Léonce in bed. Célestina was worried. In the afternoon, I closed my studio and accompanied her. When we arrived, it was actually five o'clock in the afternoon. The night was beginning to fall. Lights were burning in all the rooms of the house. Through the rain, which was coming down like mad, I thought I could see fire up there. I opened an umbrella and, with Célestina on my arm, I climbed the steep hillside. Sitting in the kitchen, a glass of rum before him, Léonce did not look so badly off. He seemed even surprised at our visit.

'Wha–wha–what is smelling so?' Célestina suddenly came out with, grabbing hold of my hand. 'So-something burning?' Following her nostrils, she went off immediately to track down the origin of the supposed fire. I ran behind her. A strange odour could really be smelt. I began to cough. Célestina stopped in front of the last door and threw it open. She retreated three steps at the sight of what awaited her. Prospère, her nephew, with a halo of a thick greyish cloud, eyes bloodshot, hair unkempt, his large gaunt frame spread out in his father Paul's bed, was smoking herb. It was a worse sight than a sugar factory at the height of the season. Célestina shut the door without a word, but I saw in her eyes a tormenting spirit on the wing and the dark foreboding of a Mona...

XI
Be More Seemly O! My Grief...

When I exhibited my photographs at Beaubourg and then in all the European capitals, I passed easily for a survivor from the shores of hell. There had been much publicity surrounding Soufrière's so-called eruption. The press had published pictures of people who were burned. Eminent vulcanologists had torn each other apart in public. Clairvoyants with international reputations had sworn that the volcano would produce thousands of victims. The firemen of Paris had been dispatched with dogs and plastic coffins.

It was in London that I met Dirk, an Anglo-Indian and a photographer like myself. His grandparents had left Amritsar in 1919, a little after the bloody shooting in the holy Sikh city. The Punjab, then the entire country, slipped into turmoil. Dirk told me ten times of their passage across an India in agony. They arrived in Madras in 1949. Only one son remained, Rajiv, and just enough to get them on to a boat that promised a life of peace in England. My Dirk was English through his mother, Margaret, whom Rajiv married in 1951. Dirk looked like Cary Grant, spoke four languages − including French − sang Verdi's *Aida* and *Rigoletto*, ate tons of ice cream without gaining an ounce, amused himself with badminton, cards and women. I could not resist him and fell, without further ado, into love's blazing fire, which burns, like dry bush, with desire, ecstasy and illusion. I had already had a few amorous encounters, known faithful admirers, tried out cohabitation. They left no mark, no scars after they ended. With Dirk, I felt hurt, anguish and torment. I waited hours for him in my hotel room, looking at the Thames flow darkly by. I cancelled an exhibition in Berlin, another in Rotterdam. I cried when he finally came and screamed when he asked me to be a little more patient. One day I licked his entire body, like a slobbering bitch. He pushed me away. I made myself ill to the point of vomiting by eating, like him, so that he would love me, quantities of ice cream. When he began to avoid me, I threatened suicide, the horror of slit veins and bloody sheets. Mad as I was, I declared my life would lose all meaning for good if he left me and hung on to his pants leg. He did not give a damn of course and slammed the door in my face. That is how he abandoned me. I remained three days crying in a stupor in my room, without drinking, without eating. One night, I telephoned Célestina. She was the one who saved me. She bought an airline ticket and headed for London, where she had never set foot; she did not even know France. She brought me back to Guadeloupe, where I wanted to die. Célestina held my hand for almost a year. I no longer was interested in anything. She dragged me along on outings to pull me out of a wave of despair that always returned to swamp me. She laughed to help me forget and came up with: 'Love can ki–kill, my dear! Without knife, without gu–gun! That's why God has always spared me...' One day, she took me to an obeahman who, from a distance, saw ghosts everywhere, under my bed, in the living room, in the kitchen. Célestina paid two thousand francs and sprinkled coloured powders in my house, hung up a crucifix, branches of God–knows–what holy bush, engravings of the Virgin, of the angel Gabriel and other benign saints. She washed me in leaves, sang me lullabies, and fed me ...

Célestina died yesterday, my good friend, my sister, my mother. Fire took her from me.

When we wake up on an ordinary day, do we know that death awaits us in the afternoon? Does some sense of dread leave us uneasy? Do we have the chance of escaping our imminent demise?

A month ago, Célestina told me: 'I had a dream. I was in a garden. But not the kind of cramped garden stuck behind houses. Nor the kind that is neglected, overrun with weeds. It was a garden full of light and colours. Look! Ju-just like this Haitian painting which brightens your bedroom wall. Fleshy fruit, heaps of vegetables, trees as massive and leafy as yo-you can imagine, twisting lianas, blooming flowers. And the sky, my dear; like a dream! Yo-you have never seen a sky like that one! Imagine a sea...Draw a beach of white sand...Put in tame, round waves like a flock of sheep...And you will see my dream sky. And, do you know who was tasting the manna from this Garden of Eden? Guess who was walking along the paths, who was putting flowers in her hair, who was picking fruits and vegetables? Me! Me, my dear!...And then I thought I saw a monkey, but it was a woman swinging through branches. I forget the shape her face. All I can tell you is that she seemed young despite her white afro, which was round like a halo. You might take her for a bride, or a communicant, an angel maybe...She was wearing long white vestments. She smiled and stretched out her hands to me. Her flesh was icy. Her smile stilled a small nagging fear in me. I let her hold on to my hand. I felt suddenly cold. Your wild imagination does not have the power to understand how I was trembling. Then, the woman began to speak. At first I did not quite get what she was saying. I politely nodded and lifted an eyebrow when she raised her tone. But, slowly, light dawned on what she was saying. At first it was words uttered at random. Then, little by little, light was shed on her entire conversation. She was saying: "Célestina! O Célestina! When war visited the earth, your papa wanted to cross the waters, poor fellow! He did not know that temptation lurking in a bottle of rum would find its way down his throat. It was a shameful day, Célestina…Do not tremble at this time, days with no fear are coming. Soon you will meet an everlasting love. The greatest of your life! And this garden in which you tread this evening is but a foretaste of the one waiting for you in the land where you are going. Forget loneliness! Be patient…love is knocking at your door." At this moment, my dear, I opened my eyes and lost the thread of the dream. What do you think of it?'

'I think you might fall in love…' That was, I think, what she wanted to hear, and, in my heart of hearts, I hoped it would be so for her (I had just met the man with whom I am today). Alas, insignificant creatures that we are, can we interpret dreams?

Two days later, a stranger rang the bell at the restaurant. At the very moment, Célestina's heart skipped a beat. She raised her head as usual, but she already knew it was he. The one she was waiting for. The man destined for her. Her lord and king; Brer

Lion on his turf. I am not talking to you about some pyaa–pyaa man that a slight gust of wind could just blow over. Don't go and imagine either some kind of not–up–to–scratch male who is in competition with women, wearing pants that were too well cut, his gestures affected and his face making you feel it was powdered. Our hero was approaching fifty. A few grey strands were sprinkled in his hair. One long wrinkle creased his forehead like the line of the horizon. His eyes had a strange glow. His slightly flared nose seemed to have smelt all the perfumes of the world. And his mouth, outlined by a black moustache, was that of an orator whom you follow to the ends of the earth, with your eyes blindfolded. Célestina did not stay rooted to one spot for long. Put yourself in her shoes! Look how long she had been waiting for him, this man first promised by Grandma Nine and then announced in a dream she had just had! Can we in our ignorance make sense of the forms which make their way through the depths of our dreams?...

Alas, Célestina herself prepared the shrimp bisque, the fried gombo and the ray stew that he ordered holding her hand all the while. The chosen one appreciated the different dishes. Célestina was delighted to catch his tongue licking his dark lips. When the banana burst into flame on his plate, our looker raised his head and looked across the unnaturally high flames of his dessert. He smiled. The poor woman grew pale and then returned the smile. The conquering hero got up and headed for the counter, where the virgin waiting to be adored stood.

'Do you like to travel, my dear lady?' he asked, running his finger along Célestina's cheek, and she purred with pleasure under the gaze of her customers, who were deeply moved. A great silence then stilled all conversation.

'I love everything that you love,' she said, without stammering.

'Then you will follow me!'

'This evening I am yours...'

'What brings you to Guadeloupe?' asked a waitress passing by.

'I am from here, my dear!' the gentleman replied.

'Do you have a garden?' inquired Célestina.

He laughed and declared: 'I have a hundred of them you can go to!'

The words they then exchanged are lost to us today. In the middle of the clinking of forks, private conversations once more filled the room. A great racket coming from the kitchen cut off, almost by design, the last words of Sir X... who, having confirmed his date, vanished.

Perhaps, if I had been at the Exotic Delight, we would not be here chatting around her coffin. Perhaps death would have gone on his way instead of seducing her. Perhaps with me she would have laughed at this Don Juan and kept her distance.

It was the first time that Léonce invited me to spend the night under his roof. When I arrived, I did not recognise the hill, clean like the face of a freshly shaved man from the woods. Seated in the rocker on the veranda, Léonce was waiting for me, his old cane in his hand.

'I have been waiting so long! You told me three o'clock, didn't you? And Célestina...'

'She couldn't make it, but she sends kisses. Who did all that?' I asked, my gaze sweeping the hillside with the infernal bush cleared.

He laughed: 'A Haitian!...They work like the Devil, those fellows! No fear of working the land. In two days, believe me, he finished off this job. You will take pictures, not so! So we don't forget...'

That evening we stayed up late talking, memories kept coming back. In defiance of taboos, he spoke to me with a frankness, surprising for his age, of the nights he spent with Myrtha in the early days of their marriage. Now, I remember how he spoke at length of Ma Octavia, with fear and respect... 'Yes, just like that, I lost the gift in a bottle of rum...Grandma never made another appearance at any of the crossroads of my life. And I do believe that I lost my mind for a long, long time. You know, the first time she came into my garden...but you could not imagine how it was transformed: fruits! flowers! great big trees with birds! You have never seen anything like it!'

I suddenly felt cold and decided to go back in. I did not sleep that night. A voice was echoing in me, swinging through the trees of a garden where death was hooting, sweeping before it a cold that makes you shiver and its drifting spirits hobbled by rusted chains. Prospère came home around three o'clock; I heard him strike one match after another until daybreak. A cock crowed as if in pain. A fine drizzle drearily began to fall. At eight o'clock, I set out on foot for the town and, soaking wet, entered the post office.

'Hello! Célestina, it's me... How are you?'

'Ah! Good morning! Is Papa ill?'

'No! Don't worry! All is fine here... Tell me, I am not hearing you clearly, how are you? You know, I thought about that dream you had and...'

'I ca–cannot talk to yo–you n–now. I am expecting someone. Call me back this evening!'

'Wait! I wanted to tell you...' She had hung up.

Those are the last words we exchanged. Her spirit was already wandering in the dim distance where love, spreading wide its sails pieced together from endlessly repeated vows, sailed across a sea smooth as glass tainted with the ink of deception.

The next day, along with Léonce, I learned from the radio about the fire at the restaurant. The firemen had found the charred body of the owner, upstairs, stretched out alone on her bed...

Afterword

> The Caribbean is not an idyll, not to its natives... Its peasantry and its fishermen are not there to be loved or even photographed; they are trees who sweat...
>
> Derek Walcott

The *Drifting of Spirits* is one of the few novels from the *Créolité* movement to appear in English. This literary movement has been for the past ten years the only noteworthy one in the entire Caribbean. It has produced novelists of great distinction, such as Patrick Chamoiseau and Raphael Confiant. The French Caribbean has not seen such a literary renaissance since the flowering of Negritude with the poetry of Aimé Cesaire in the late 1930s. The achievement of this school of writing received its highest recognition in 1992, when Chamoiseau was awarded the Prix Goncourt for his novel *Texaco*. In the following year *The Drifting of Spirits*, Gisèle Pineau's first important novel, received the Prix Carbet and, in 1994, *Le prix des lecteurs d'Elle*.

The *Créolité* movement is centred in Martinique, one of the French Overseas Departments in the Caribbean. These departments, Martinique, Guadeloupe and French Guyana, have been French possessions since 1635 and have had a largely unbroken relationship with the mother country. In 1946, they voted to become departments of France. This decision led not only to the loss of political autonomy but also to chronic economic dependence and cultural erosion. Fifty years after departmentalisation, the agricultural base, as well as any self-sustaining productivity in these territories, especially in Martinique, is fast disappearing because of rapid urbanisation and the spread of consumer culture. The *Créolité* movement is, as much as anything, a response to the progressive disappearance of a cultural hinterland and the fear of being swamped by the reductive universalism and homogenisation that departmental status has brought.

Créolité is essentially a strategic defence of the ideal of diversity in a world threatened by the disappearance of cultural difference. Such a threat is acutely felt by artists and intellectuals in Martinique, where total integration into the metropolitan system has been the legacy of departmentalisation. The idea of cultural difference proposed by *Créolité* and derived from their main theorist, the Martinican writer Edouard Glissant, is different from earlier theories of racial or national identity that have prevailed in the Caribbean region. Glissant posited a more open-ended form of identity in his theoretical work *Caribbean Discourse* published in 1981. A French Caribbean identity in particular and a Caribbean specificity in general were conceived not in terms of an exclusive or regressive model but rather as an unpredictable, integrating, ongoing process of Creolisation. Old ideals of *marronage* and resistance were replaced by strategies of integration, fusion and opposition within a context of contact and consent.

Novelists of the *Créolite* school have used this model to scrutinise previously overlooked areas of French Caribbean culture. No other cultural phenomenon has, perhaps, received more attention in this regard than the Creole language itself. They do not attempt to faithfully transcribe the Creole spoken by the majority of French Caribbean people. Instead, they approach the Creole language as an interlect, a linguistic code which is constructed around exchange, interference, accommodation and transformation. The language of their novels does not, therefore, aspire to a monolingual authenticity but to a creative linguistic disorder which ranges from pure Creole utterances through Creole-based neologisms to standard French. It is this capacity for a dynamic and creative code-switching that has become the hallmark of fiction which always strives to give the impression that it is spoken rather than written, which invariably invokes the storyteller and directly addresses the reader. It is precisely this capacity for experimentation that prompted an admiring Milan Kundera to say in 1991 that Patrick Chamoiseau 'takes liberties with French which not one of his French contemporaries could even imagine ever taking'.

The major practitioners of *Créolite* since 1986 have been male and Martinican. Gisèle Pineau is female and Guadeloupean. Unlike the other *Créolistes*, she did not grow up in the Caribbean but was born in exile among the hundreds of thousands of French West Indians living in France. She is also unusual because she does not have the French university background shared by her contemporaries. She abandoned her university education for financial reasons, trained as a psychiatric nurse and has been practising her profession in Guadeloupe since 1980. This choice of profession, as well as her longings as an outsider for a culture and space of her own has no doubt left its mark on her writing. In any case, her sensitivity would inevitably be shaped by the stronger sense of a local identity that exists in Guadeloupe as opposed to the much more assimilated neighbouring island of Martinique.

The Drifting of Spirits is a story which can be enjoyed on a number of levels. It is a love story, a family saga and the evocation of life in a community called Haute-Terre, as much as a wry account of how an outsider comes to terms with a world she can see only as picturesque, a montage of oddities that belongs on a museum wall. Judging by this novel, Pineau's literary influences must be quite diverse. There is enough of the minutiae and miscellany of everyday existence evoked in concrete detail to suggest an affinity with the nineteenth-century French 'naturalist' Emile Zola. Yet there is also an interest in myth, in the belief systems of a community and, most importantly, in the enigmatic lives of women to bring to mind a controversial female novelist and anthropologist from the Harlem Renaissance, Zora Neale Hurston. Yet, beyond the influences of Zola and Zora, Pineau brings to her fiction an impressive sensitivity to the ironies of human behaviour, as well as a precise ear for the speech, the beliefs and the world view of her native Guadeloupe.

Derek Walcott warns of the perils of development that risk turning writers into folklorists. This risk of a self-indulgent nostalgia is very real for the *Créolité* movement, as local culture increasingly becomes a spectacle, given the overdeveloped nature of the island departments and the pervasiveness of Europeanization. Pineau's narrator is a photographer who can scarcely resist the temptation to collect, embellish and repackage the world and the people around her. Her initial impulse is to see the rural inhabitants as Plato's unregenerate cavedwellers, whereas her authority comes from her camera's flash of light. Her greatest successes are the photographs of those fleeing the explosions of La Soufrière volcano. Yet she cannot photograph the world of the spirits or the ways of the occult that determine the exits and entrances of the characters in this tale. If a pictoral representation exists of their world, it is in the marvellous world of Haiti's intuitive painters, whose art seems to hover behind the evocation of the lives of the people of Haute-Terre.

The authority of the photographer/narrator is contested not only at this level but also in terms of her condescending attitude to the behaviour and beliefs of those around her. For instance, female behaviour in this story is often mysterious and unpredictable. Women do odd things with their lives. They stay with men who beat them and are compulsively unfaithful. The men to whom they sacrifice their lives are not always real. A schoolteacher, despite her identification with women's liberation, loses her heart and mind to a diabolical spirit named Victor Hugo. The narrative actually ends with Célestina's assignation with death, who appears as an irresistibly well-mannered, handsome gentleman, the incarnation of Baron Samedi, the Haitian god of the graveyard. Yet the progressive, liberated photographer herself, as she confesses, is equally prone to irrational behaviour and self-debasement for the sake of love. If anything, this story is an initiation of the female narrator into the world of her native informants and the fatalism that controls their lives.

The tale is divided into two parts which derive

their names from a saying known throughout the Caribbean – 'What goes around, comes around.' The pattern of repeated cycles, of rise and fall, dominates the tale. Time is marked in the story by disaster. The three main 'historical' events that frame the lives of these characters are the hurricane of 1928, the Second World War and the eruption of La Soufrière in 1976. In the same way that they have no control over these 'natural' disasters, they are equally subject to physical characteristics that determine their futures. Léonce's physical deformity is an abiding source of insecurity, as the voice in his head constantly reminds him. His father-in-law, Sosthène, is equally beset by his insatiable sexual needs. Célestina's stammering leads inexorably to her demise. On the other hand, France's beauty ensures her success in a local beauty contest and later as an international model.

The spirits may drift in this tale but the characters are housed, both literally in their intricately designed cabins and symbolically in their extended family structures. The main family group with which the story deals is that of Ninette and Sosthène, who have three children, Léonce, Hector and Lucina. The events are centred on the experiences of Léonce, who marries Myrtha, one of a pair of twins, and their family of four children, Célestina, the twins, Paul and Céluta, and Gerty. The novel comes to a close with a fourth generation, the children of Paul and the long-suffering Romaine who are named France and Prospère. The love story of Léonce and Myrtha holds the plot together and Léonce's garden seems to be the centre of narrative. It is a garden of encounter, revelation, courtship, longing and, eventually, decay, an infallible index to the fortunes and mental states of the main characters.

Although Guadeloupe's dependence on France is apparent, particularly in the celebrations to mark the tricentenary of island's relationship with the mother country in 1935, this does not mean that Pineau's characters are simply casualties of Guadeloupe's colonial and later pseudo-colonial status. As the voyeuristic narrator must eventually learn, these people are complete, complex individuals whose universe is totally coherent, despite the scepticism of the uninitiated outsider. In this regard, the novel requires the reader to be patient and suspend moral judgement not only with regard to behaviour and beliefs but also in terms of the language of the text. This translation attempts to be as faithful as possible to the language of the original, which did not provide the French reader with a glossary; nor was any attempt made to bowdlerize the text and expurgate the references to genitalia and sexual activity with which male and female characters are equally preoccupied. Most of all, the original text is marked by a pervasive sense of humour. Lives and worlds collide in this novel not only tragically but also in outrageously funny and playful ways. The English translation, in an effort to capture the liveliness or bawdiness of Pineau's linguistically inventive narrative, often contains words and expressions from what might be termed Caribbean English. Most of all, like the best fiction from the *Créolite* movement, Pineau's very Guadeloupean text spoke directly to the French reader. It can only be hoped that this English version has as much to say to an anglophone audience.

I would like to thank Gisèle Pineau for her assistance with this translation. The advice of Lina Williams and, most of all, the help of Stella Vincent were invaluable in the production of the final version of the typescript.

J.M.D.